# GREAT ROBOTS
# OF HISTORY

Black Shuck Books
www.blackshuckbooks.co.uk

First published in Great Britain in 2025 by
Black Shuck Books
Kent, UK

Versions of the following stories have previously appeared in print:
'Wax Caesar Displaying His 23 Wounds to the Crowd' in *Cthonic Matter vol. 1 issue 4* (2023)
'The Andraiad' in *Interzone 290/291* (2021)
'Echec!' as a standalone chapbook (Salò Press, 2024)
'The Brazen Head of Westinghouse' in *IZ Digital* (2023)
'Degrees of Freedom' in *Shoreline of Infinity #38* (2024)
'Dear Will' in *Vastarien vol. 3 issue 2* (2020)
'Four Fabrications of Francine Descartes' in *Saros #1* (2025)
'The Cardboard Voice' in *Nightscript vol. 7* (2021)
'There Goes the Neighbourhood' in *Abyss & Apex #92* (2024)
'The Horizon' in *Nonbinary Review #36* (2024)

Set in Caslon
Cover & interior design © WHITEspace, 2025
www.white-space.uk

978-1-917173-05-6

# Great Robots of History

by

## Tim Major

BLACK
SHUCK
BOOKS

*For Joe and Arthur*

# | Contents |

~

# |The Funnel|

~

The journalist shuddered visibly as he took off his coat and leant his folded umbrella against the coatrack in the entrance hall. Over his shoulder Faye could see that it was barely drizzling outside.

"Are you cold?" she asked.

Her visitor considered the question for longer than seemed necessary. "Not especially. It's fairly warm in here."

"It takes an age to heat this old building. And a small fortune."

They passed through the high-ceilinged hall. The journalist's voice echoed as he asked, "Does your department take up the entire building?"

"No. But the other wings are used mainly for storage. I'm as remote and sequestered here as it's possible to be in Cambridge."

Faye showed him into a small lounge containing a horseshoe of low, faded red couches. Affixed to the rear wall was a melamine counter with a water heater and a few boxes containing tea, coffee and biscuits.

The journalist glanced at the nearest couch, but didn't sit. He extended his hand to Faye. "It's a pleasure to meet you. My name's Kelvin Freed."

"Of?"

"Pardon?"

"Your employer. I'm not sure I caught the name of the newspaper when you called."

"Oh. The *Echo*."

She smiled. "Of course. You must be dying for a cuppa." Even to her own ears, the phrase still carried a note of falsity, or at least of rehearsal, despite her many years living in England.

Kelvin nodded.

"I don't drink caffeine," Faye said, "and I'm hopeless at judging the strength. Would you mind helping yourself?"

Kelvin hesitated, then moved to the counter, lifting lids and peering inside. After a few false starts he succeeded in drawing hot water from the nozzle of the wall-mounted machine. He dipped the teabag three times, removed it and dropped it onto a plate where other sodden teabags lay heaped. Then he looked around, perhaps searching for milk. Finally, he placed the mug on the counter, the drink as yet untasted.

"Shall we get straight to it, then?" Faye asked.

"Yes, let's."

She sat on one of the couches and Kelvin took a position almost, but not quite, opposite her. It seemed an interesting impulse.

"First," he said, "I'd like to know a little about you."

Faye raised an eyebrow.

"Is something wrong?" he asked.

"No. I just thought you'd have brought a Dictaphone, or at least a notepad."

He smiled and tapped his forehead. "It's safe up here."

"You have a good memory?"

"Outstanding. I'm known for it."

"I've never read your column. What's it about?"

"It's called 'Freed Speech'." He acknowledged her grimace. "I know, I know. But I was determined to get my surname into the title. I specialise in human-interest stories."

"I see. And why do I qualify?"

Kelvin tapped an index finger on his chin. "That's what I'm here to find out."

"Very well. My name is Dr Faye Molyneux. I suppose it's clear I'm not from around here, originally."

"You're French?"

"Among other things. I've worked here at the Dippel Foundation for six years, though I operated it more informally before that."

"I don't understand. Does that mean you created the foundation yourself?"

She laughed. "I *am* the foundation. In fact, this is the greatest number of people that has been present in this room – in this building – since I began." She gestured at the ring of couches. "This place used to be a proper university department, and I haven't bothered to clear out the old stuff. I've been too focused on other things."

"Why do you need such a large building?"

"For my other things."

"What's the nature of your work here?"

"How much do you know already?"

"Nothing at all."

"Then how did you come across my name?"

The journalist waved a hand. "Someone in the office mentioned you, I think. I tend to follow hunches. I trust in the universe to guide me."

"You trust in the universe to guide you," Faye repeated. "How interesting."

"Is that so strange?"

"I mean… do you *really* believe that?"

Kelvin pursed his lips. "No, not really. It's just something you say, isn't it?"

"That's a relief. I was beginning to think you were a… how can I put it? A crank."

They stared at one another in silence for several seconds.

Then Faye stood, went to the counter and fished a crumbling biscuit from a tin. "How about I show you some examples of my work, to avoid this awkwardness we've somehow created?"

Faye liked the building to be heated continually throughout, yet she turned off lights whenever she left a room. Everybody has their inconsistencies.

When she flicked on the light of the first chamber, she was pleased to note Kelvin's intake of breath.

The windows of the room were shuttered, and the room itself was almost featureless apart from several schematic diagrams blu-tacked to the walls – and the large, skeletal structure in the centre of the space. Faye watched the journalist, whose attention was occupied with the large cogs within the hollow box that comprised the base of the structure, before his gaze rose and settled on the spindly metal bird perched on top of it.

"Is that a duck?" Kelvin asked.

"Not just any duck."

"I suppose not. It's a metal duck. A golden duck."

"Have you ever seen it before?"

"Of course not."

"It isn't a silly question. This duck is famous. Or at least it was."

"It looks like something Leonardo da Vinci might have made."

"Very good, Mr Freed."

He turned sharply to look at her. "Is it?"

"Is it a da Vinci? No. I've got his mechanical knight upstairs, but it's not suitable for display. It's come down with a bug."

He hesitated before saying, "You're joking."

"Very astute. Which part was the joke?"

"The bug. Mechanical things don't have bugs, only living organisms. Or computers, I suppose." He peered at the duck again. "What does this thing actually do?"

Faye bent to a flywheel attached to the base of the structure and turned it six times. The larger wheels within the box began to spin slowly, whereupon the attached cams bumped several followers up and down in sequence. Faye stood back and held up her hand, palm flat. Upon it were the crumbs that remained of her biscuit.

After emitting a series of clicks that made Faye wince, the neck of the golden duck arched, and its beak dabbed into her hand. It pushed at the crumbs until it succeeded in scooping up one of the larger chunks, at which point its neck flexed in the opposite direction in a fair mimicry of swallowing.

"That's terrific," Kelvin said, with what seemed genuine enthusiasm.

"Hold on. She's not finished yet."

The duck produced an odd muffled sound that hardly seemed mechanical.

"Put your hand there," she said, pointing, "near its rear end."

Kelvin complied.

"Palm up."

He did as instructed.

More gulping sounds came from within the duck. Its golden body shook slightly. Then, with a faint scraping noise, something dropped from its rear and into Kelvin's open hand.

He withdrew it sharply, staring at the moist, greenish substance.

"Sorry," Faye said.

He stared at her blankly.

She pulled a tissue from the pocket of her jacket and offered it to him. Even when he had rubbed the shit away, he kept rubbing.

"It's not real, you know," she said, watching his response carefully.

He stopped, then raised the tissue to his nose and sniffed.

"It's not even made from the same biscuit crumbs," she went on. "It's breadcrumbs and green dye."

"Oh. Then it's a trick. What for?"

"To amaze, of course. And it did, back in 1739."

Kelvin looked at the machine anew. "It's really that old?"

Ignoring the question, Faye went on. "It was built by Jacques de Vaucanson, and it was a sensation. It's had quite a life since then. Long after it was exhibited, it found its way into the hands of Jean-Eugène Robert-Houdin. Heard of him?"

"Is that Houdini, the magician?"

"A common mistake. Houdini was a stage name adopted as a tribute. Anyway, it's unimportant. Would you like to see another machine? Do you think that'd be of interest to readers of your column?"

Kelvin nodded uncertainly.

Faye flicked off the lights.

The journalist watched the wooden snail edge jerkily across the table. Its shell was scratched and worn.

"I call foul," he said.

Faye smiled indulgently. "Why's that?"

"You said it was displayed at the Dionysia festival in Athens. But you also mentioned a parade. This is tiny. And—" He pursed his lips in thought. "It's a myth, surely. Even if it wasn't, nothing like this could survive from as long ago as 308 BC."

"You've caught me out."

"It's impressive, all the same. If it's not really old, can I touch it?"

She bowed her head.

When Kelvin plucked the snail from the tabletop, its mechanism continued to whirr. He turned it upside-down, exposing the two drive wheels and single front wheel. Something shifted heavily. The snail emitted a shrill squeak.

Kelvin dropped it with a clatter, then gasped again as the wooden shell split into two on impact. Now the internal treadmill was visible, along with the white mouse that had been powering it.

"Surprise," Faye said drily. "Like Demetrios of Phaleron, the creator of the snail, I've concluded that there are multiple ways to achieve a desired effect."

"Please don't take this question the wrong way," Kelvin said, "but how have you managed to get funding for all this? I do understand that these automatons are of historical significance, or at least they would be if they were the real, authentic ones—"

Faye cut him off. "That's a key issue. Realism and authenticity were the two driving ambitions of the creators of these machines, though of course they achieved neither. But you're saying that the original models would have possessed those characteristics?"

"I only mean as historical artifacts."

Faye considered this as she moved along the dim corridor, then retrieved a key from her pocket and placed it in the lock of a nondescript door.

"I'd like to know more about the Dippel Foundation," Kelvin said behind her. "What is its aim?"

"The same as it's been for three hundred years."

"I thought you created it."

"Did I say that?"

"That's what I understood you to mean. If not you, then who did?"

"Johann Konrad Dippel. Who just happens to be my great-great-great-and-several-more-greats-grandfather, on my mother's side. Heard of him?"

"No."

"How bothersome. It's my only real claim to fame. Why *were* you sent to speak to me, I wonder?"

She opened the door before he could reply. Immediately, a dog began barking from within. When she tried to usher Kelvin inside, he didn't move.

"It won't bite," she said. "Or at least it's never bitten anyone before now."

She watched the journalist as he entered the room, noting his wince, his fumbling for the light switch, then his double-take, the rapid blinking of his eyes, the slackening of his facial features as he found a source of reassurance. As she followed him inside the room, the dog continued to snarl and bark, shaking its iron head and arching its back in response to the movement of complex gears that could be glimpsed within its body. Two of its feet – the left front one and the rear right – were capable of lifting from the flat base to give the illusion of life, but the others were fixed in place.

"Who—" Kelvin began, then he gulped as if to clear a tightness in his throat. "Who made this one?"

"Unknown. But it's said it guarded the palace of Alcinous, the King of Phaeacia, along with its twin."

"Not really, though."

"No, not really."

Kelvin turned to face her. Each time the dog barked, his eyes narrowed.

"What's the point?" he asked.

"Human interest," Faye replied blandly.

"But you said nobody comes here. Do you exhibit these machines?"

She shook her head.

"This man Dippel – the original. He did this too? He created mechanical animals?"

"Not mechanical ones, no."

Kelvin frowned in confusion. "You say that as though he created *non*-mechanical ones."

"No, not that either."

"Dr Molyneux, I'm afraid this is starting to become—"

"Annoying?"

"No. It's just that I don't know how much of this I can use."

"Ah, your column. 'Freed Speech'." Faye laughed lightly. She moved to the window and drew one of the heavy shutters aside. "Did you take a taxi to get here, or did you walk from the station?"

He took a moment to reply. "I drove."

"There's no car outside."

He joined her at the window to survey the small car park, which was empty. Faye didn't own a car herself, and she lived in the rooms at the very top of this wing of the building.

"I parked nearby," Kelvin said. "I fancied the walk."

"In the rain."

"Yes. I don't mind it. I like the feel of rain on my face."

"An odd decision to carry an umbrella, then."

Kelvin didn't reply.

Faye closed the shutter again, sharply. She pointed at the dog, which now only produced low snarls, as if it had become accustomed to their presence but still didn't trust them.

"I wonder if you would consider it more authentic," she said, "if it *believed* it was the original dog that had guarded the Phaeacian palace?" Then, without waiting for an answer, she said, "Come on. Let's check on the kids."

"The nursery is the only room I permit to be lit at all times," she said as she pushed at the door. "If I leave them in darkness, the wailing becomes most distracting, even when I'm on the ground floor."

She paused with the door only half open. "Out of interest, what are you expecting to see in here?"

Kelvin's face was impressively pale. "I'm tempted to give a gruesome answer, as if this was a scene from a horror story. But I think there are more automatons in there."

Despite his statement, he blanched even more as the door swung fully open.

Each of the children sat within a glass case, each at his own desk, bare feet and pudgy toes visible beneath. Their pens scratched furiously upon sheets of paper. The boys were almost identical, though familiarity allowed Faye to perceive differences in the shade of their hair, the elaborateness of their neck ruffs, the ruddiness of their cheeks.

"What do you think of them?" she asked.

Cautiously, Kelvin edged forward, then bent to the level of the children, examining the papers that contained the results of their work. Ordinarily, the draughtsman produced portraits of Louis XV. The writer was busy producing a sequence of letters – it was capable of up to forty in length.

Kelvin still crouched before the children, entirely motionless.

"Is something the matter?" Faye asked in genuine concern.

Kelvin only gestured vaguely at the cases. Faye moved to stand alongside him so that she could see the work that the children had produced. The writer's effort was a shorter message than usual:

*I Will Cheer You to the Echo*

Most interesting. An echo of an echo. As Faye wondered whether this apparent coincidence might have affected Kelvin adversely, she glanced at the draughtsman's desk. Rather than Louis XV, it had produced a passable rendering of the face of Kelvin Freed himself. As far as Faye could tell, the child had completed its work before she and the journalist had entered the room.

To her surprise, Kelvin made no comment, as if had recognised himself in neither work. He only raised his hand to the glass case that enclosed the draughtsman.

Abruptly, the boy raised its head. Kelvin gasped and fell backwards onto the floorboards. When he didn't seem able to rise, Faye helped him up.

"His eyes," Kelvin said in a shaking voice.

"What about them?"

"He looked at me."

"You mean its eyes moved to track your location."

"No. Something more than that. I can't say it any other way. They *looked* at me."

Faye folded her arms over her chest. "Then I take it you're impressed?"

"That's not the word I'd have used. More like… I don't know. How did it do that?"

"Both machines are immensely complex. The draughtsman comprises two thousand constituent elements, the writer six thousand. They predate Babbage's Difference Engine, would you believe."

"No. I don't mean any of that. I mean…" He peered at each child in turn. They had stopped scribbling and now both of their faces were raised, their eyes following his movements minutely.

"I understand," Faye said. "It all comes back to Dippel. He had no expertise in automatons, but he would certainly have relished all these demonstrations. His field of research related to the soul. You've really never heard of him?"

Kelvin shook his head.

"The name of his home ought to be familiar, though." She adopted a spooky tone. "Castle Frankenstein."

The journalist stared at her.

"I'm serious," she said. "Dippel was born there – it's a real castle, near Darmstadt in Germany. At university he studied the usual – theology, philosophy, anatomy, alchemy – and continued his research afterwards. His specialism was soul-transference from one cadaver to another, using what he described rather reductively as a 'funnel'." She laughed. "I know what you're thinking! What's the point? It's not much use putting a soul in another body that's as dead as the first one. But I suppose you have to start somewhere." She examined Kelvin's blank expression, trying to gauge his response. "You know, it still puzzles me that you don't use a notebook. Are you going to remember all this?"

"Yes," Kelvin said with certainty.

"Funnily enough, a certain Mary Shelley once saw these same units," Faye said, gesturing at the watching children. "You can imagine they made an impression on her."

The journalist gave no sign of recognition. Was it possible he had never heard of Mary Shelley, or *Frankenstein*? It seemed a peculiar omission, even for someone who defined himself as only a mediocre journalist at a mediocre local newspaper. He'd gone too far.

Kelvin raised a hand to his forehead. Even though it was dry, he mopped at it thoughtlessly using the tissue still clutched in his hand, which was soiled with artificial duck shit.

"Are you quite all right, Mr Freed?"

"They're real," he said.

"Meaning what? What is real? What is authenticity?"

His eyes were wide, almost wild. Faye was transfixed at this demonstration of his wide range of expressions.

"They're alive," he said in a hoarse tone.

She snorted softly. "I can just imagine you screaming that in triumph, like in the James Whale film: 'It's alive!'"

Again, he displayed no sign of recognition.

"Dr Molyneux—"

"Yes, Mr Freed?"

"What do you really do here?"

"I continue the work of the foundation – that is, the work of Johann Konrad Dippel."

"But it's nonsense. All this talk of transferring souls. This idea of a... a *funnel*."

"You're quite correct," she said to Kelvin. "Then let's dispense of the theatrics. There's no harnessing of lightning involved, no literal funnels to pour souls from one body to another. These boys aren't alive, as I am. But you're also correct that they're special. Their creator, Pierre Jaquet-Droz, may have been a genius, but even he wouldn't have claimed he had given his children minds or consciousnesses."

Kelvin seemed to be absorbing this. After a few seconds, he said, "And what about you, Dr Molyneux? Would you claim to have done so?"

"Perhaps." She studied the journalist for several seconds, then shook her head. "No. Not yet. But what begins as an illusion can be made increasingly complex, until the distinction between illusion and life is so subtle as to be barely relevant. Look – a magician never reveals her secrets, but I make no claims of being a magician either. I'm just having my fun. So I'll tell you. Most of the automata you've seen this afternoon, and those in storage, are just the products of a hobby. But the dog and this industrious pair of children are a little different. They really do experience the world around them, because they've been recipients of the funnel."

In a choked voice, Kelvin said, "But you just conceded there *is* no funnel."

"No physical funnel, I meant. And no cadaver acting as a donor, either. It's simply a process, bestowing upon the recipient a state that you may or may not choose to call life. I can assure you it's nothing that isn't being done elsewhere, though the emphasis tends to vary from institution to institution. Have you had a chance to dabble with any of the AI chatbots online? The principal is somewhat similar."

"I'm sorry, I don't know what you mean."

She nodded. "There do seem to be odd blind spots in your knowledge today. Then again, you haven't claimed to have a technology background, or any literary or cultural awareness, for that matter. It's as if you've deliberately closed yourself off from certain aspects of standard knowledge, to suit your role. You've turned rather pale, Mr Freed. Would you like some water?"

"No, thank you," he said quickly.

"I suppose not. I do hope you'll be safe to drive."

Weakly, he said, "Yes. Yes, in fact I think I ought to be getting along now."

"So soon? Do you feel you've gathered enough information for your column?"

"Yes. I think so. I must go home." As if it was an afterthought, he said quietly, "My wife. My children."

It was peculiar that he hadn't mentioned them before, but perhaps the children in glass boxes had struck more of a chord than Faye had realised, prompting this new association. Kelvin moved unsteadily to the door of the nursery, and she followed him, ignoring the plaintive moans from within the glass cases. She considered turning off the light after all, to teach the children a lesson about upsetting people, then thought better of it.

"What will your angle be, in the article?" she asked Kelvin. "Artificial intelligence?"

He stopped on the uppermost step of the staircase, considering the question. "I liked the duck very much," he said. Then he added, "Is that really all that's behind the trick, then? A computer program that makes automatons appear lifelike?"

Faye bowed her head. "Though the real 'trick', as you call it, is that the recipients themselves are taken in by it." Her gaze drifted to the closed door of the nursery. One of the children called out, but she couldn't tell whether Kelvin had heard it. In general, he seemed rather stunned by his experience. She went on, "I do sometimes wonder whether there's cruelty in what I do. Whether the illusion of discomfort, in somebody who themselves is only an illusion, may be as bad as the real thing."

Then she gathered herself and said brightly, "I hope you'll send me a copy of the article?"

"Yes," Kelvin said in a voice that was barely more than a whisper. "Before or after publication?"

She smiled. She found it charming that he still believed he worked for the *Echo*, or that the *Echo* even existed.

"Either will do," she said.

Downstairs in the entrance hall, Kelvin looked blankly at his coat on the rack, then at the umbrella leaning against it. It was as if he didn't recognise them. He patted his pockets, perhaps expecting to find car keys there, but his flustered manner suggested he'd come up short.

"Is anything the matter, Mr Freed?" Faye asked pleasantly. It would be irresponsible to let him go out into the rain, which had now become a downpour. He mightn't survive. "Would you prefer to come back inside and sit down for a moment?"

As he turned to face her, his eyes were wide, suggesting fear. His pale cheeks twitched continually and most unnaturally. Work was needed.

"I think I better had," he said. "It's the strangest thing. I can't seem to remember where I live."

# |Wax Caesar Displaying His 23 Wounds to the Crowd|

**Name:** Roland Morris
**Class:** 11L
**Project title:** Wax Caesar Displaying His 23 Wounds to the Crowd

**Learning objective:** *To bring a key moment of history to life through research and presentation*

In order to bring a key moment of history to life, you first have to ask yourself: what is history? It is an uncountable noun that refers to the events of the past.

*[Finish introduction later]*

There are lots of ways you could bring history to life. Some are more difficult than others, like building a time machine! Or zombies. Some people in Class 11L think that drawing a big picture is bringing history to life, but it isn't. Writing a story does, just about, but you have to be quite good at it, otherwise it's just words on a page.

The best way to bring history to life is by acting it out. I went to Drama camp last summer, and at the end we got to perform a thing at the Theatre Royal, and when the audience (meaning the teachers and the kids who did lighting instead of acting) clapped at the end, they clapped loudest for me because I was *funny* and didn't just read out my lines like a robot. The script didn't even tell me to pretend not to be able to open the front door in Act 1, but that's what I did, for *ages*, and it got funnier every second. So I know what I'm talking about.

Meera and Lucy R said they wanted to do acting too, but when I asked if I could join their group they just ignored me. Callum and Isaac and Jeong said they already knew what scene they were going to do and there were only three people in it. But history is *full* of people, every bit of it.

Anyway, I ended up with Nick.

Nick's all right. It depends where you meet him. He's weird in break times, for instance. He just stares. But in class he sort of comes alive. Maybe that's why I said yes when he asked if we could be partners, because 'alive' was what I needed. Nick's more alive than Meera or Lucy R, when he wants to be.

### Project team and roles:
- Roland Morris (project lead, researcher, set designer, voice actor, actor)
- Nick Warren (actor)

### Choosing a historic period:
The best period of history is Ancient Rome. And the Prohibition in America. In 1930s Chicago they wore striped suits, not just the gangsters but also the customers at the speakeasies, and striped suits are hard to get. In Ancient Rome they wore basically sheets and curtains. That's not why Ancient Rome is the best historic period but it is practical.

Me and Nick agreed that we should do Ancient Rome. Right away we both said Julius Caesar and then we both said jinx. Saying jinx meant neither of us could say anything else until... Well, that's the trouble. Nobody agrees what you have to do to get rid of a jinx. So me and Nick sat there saying nothing until Miss Lynch told us to stop being daft and crack on.

I said that Caesar conquering Gaul would be best. We could do Caesar in his war room, moving horses around, and we could use knights from chess sets. It would be really funny. Caesar would be planning the attack on some part of Gaul, and then he'd climb up onto the table with all the towns marked on it with models, and he'd go stamping around on the table, squashing the cardboard houses and castles, shouting all the time. Man, that would be *funny*. You wouldn't need anybody except Caesar. I could have done it all on my own.

Nick said no. He said something about pacifism and something about Asterix and something about visual impact. At the start of the project I didn't always listen carefully to what he said.

Nick said that the death of Caesar was best.

I mean, it's a good idea, it really is. We did Julius Caesar in Year 10 – meaning the Shakespeare play, not that we *did* Julius Caesar, ha ha. I bet Lucy R would, though. *[Delete?]*

So we chose the death of Caesar. I said I'd be Caesar because it was my project, and Nick stared at me for ages and then he said okay but in a weird quiet voice.

The trouble was that there was only two of us. That's one Julius Caesar and one Brutus. But then what about the senators? There were like 100 of them *[Check on Wikipedia]* that all killed Caesar together. Two would be okay. But we didn't even have two other people.

Then I had this great idea. I said we could paint the senators onto a background, all spitting and eyes rolling and that sort of thing. Then we'd only need Caesar and Brutus. And if we were doing a picture then we could even have this flap that flapped down when I got stabbed, and behind the flap is this picture of Caesar's ghost flying up to Mount Olympus, but not that, the Roman one. With gods and everything. How good would that be?

Nick said okay but still in that weird voice, and with too many 'o's. I said do you have a better idea? And he said I didn't mean the stabbing in the Senate. I meant the funeral.

I said what? I said funerals aren't fun. I said funerals aren't bringing history to life, are they?

Nick just went quiet and stared, like he does at break times. Even when Miss Lynch told us off again he just stared. After a while I couldn't handle it anymore. I said okay but with even more 'o's than he used, just to show him how I really felt.

That's how we chose the funeral of Caesar.

### Research:

> *[Do research and put it here, with pictures and everything.]*

### Developing the presentation:

Nick said he knew loads about the funeral of Caesar. He said he'd read a whole book. After the first planning lesson he went away and drew all these pictures and brought them back for me to look at. They were actually pretty good but I can't include them in my project folder because later Nick burned almost all of them and one of them he actually ate, right in front of me.

It doesn't matter because I can describe them, because they were all basically the same. Mark Antony is on the left, doing his funeral speech. The crowd of people is on the right, with their mouths wide open in shock and getting pissed off ready to riot. *[Not pissed off. Words from thesaurus.com: exasperated irate outraged impassioned.]* The part that changed in each of Nick's pictures was Caesar. Not *the* Caesar, because he's dead at this point, obviously. He's not even in the scene, really – maybe just his cold dead feet off to one side. The Caesar you can see is the effigy of Caesar that Mark Antony made. It was made of wax but mechanical somehow. The wax Caesar is on a sort of box above the crowds and there's curly arrows showing how he rotates when a handle is turned. It's wax Caesar that the crowd are looking up at.

When Nick said I could be Caesar it was a trick, because that was when I thought we were doing his death in the Senate. I'm excellent at deaths, like when I was old Ben Gunn in *Treasure Island*, which was so *funny*. But there's a difference between dying and being dead. So I said to Nick I wanted to be Mark Antony because he gets to do the whole speech and then reveal the wax Caesar and then say let's riot.

Nick said sure, okay, really quick this time.

We started making the background. I'm excellent at painting and I can even do faces, but when I started sketching people in the crowd Nick got angry and turned the paper over to the blank side. He said we won't need them. Then he saw that I was exasperated irate outraged impassioned and he said okay, do some statues, they're people, aren't they.

Nick told Miss Lynch that our scene would be big and so after the half-term holiday could we have the little Drama workshop to ourselves, and she said yes but she'd check in on us every quarter of an hour. Even Miss Lynch knew that Nick was weird sometimes, even back then.

In the half-term holiday I finished the big background picture. I didn't take a photo of it and now it's too singed to see much of the statues or the stone columns. For the costumes my dad gave me some old sheets and even two halves of a curtain, but the curtains had flowers on so I said no.

I don't know how Nick got into school out of term time, but he must have. History was second period on the Monday back, and I was with him in Biology before that. Anyway, when I went into the little Drama workshop it was already full of people.

Not real people, though. They were shop dummies.

I stood and looked at them all and I said what? Just that, again and again. What?

Nick said how many robes did you get. I mean sheets. I said two, one for you and one for me. He said we will need more.

The dummies weren't meant to be the wax Caesar, you see. The dummies were the crowd. I mean, it makes sense. It's quite a good idea, if you have enough dummies, which we did, and enough sheets, which we didn't. I said I don't have enough sheets. Do you want me to steal sheets from the beds of my family? Nick just stared at me and I don't even know if it meant yes or no or something else. We spend the lesson sticking up the background picture and making the platform for Mark Antony. When we finished I realised we wouldn't be able to get it out of the little Drama workshop, which is why it's still in there.

I don't know where the other sheets came from. All I know is the next History lesson the dummies were all dressed. I hardly even noticed the sheets at first, though. I was looking at the faces. I suppose they're papier-mâché. Nick can't be any good at papier-mâché, because the faces are all lumpy, with their noses too long and just holes for eyes, and all painted white like he wasn't even trying to make them look real. More like dead clowns.

I stood on the platform to see how it would feel to be Mark Antony. It felt weird, mainly because of the dead-eyed clowns. Nick watched for a while and kept giving me advice. He didn't say anything about my speech, though. He just said things like (i) lift your right arm up; (ii) sort of snarl; (iii) bring fire into your eyes.

Then Nick stood on this box to be the effigy of Caesar. I said what happened to your sheet because it was all ripped up. He said it has to be ripped. He said the wax Caesar was created by Mark Antony in order to show Julius Caesar's 23 wounds to the crowd. If they can't see the 23 wounds, they won't riot. I looked at the crowd of clowns and thought about them all rioting and I shuddered and then I said whatever, Nick.

Nick must have been working away at the project the whole half-term holiday. Otherwise how could he have made the box lift up above the crowd like that? I don't even know how it works or what Nick did to make it start going up. When it was above the heads of the crowd it started turning around. The heads of the dummies moved like they were watching it, which gave me a massive shock. I guess there are strings attached to them somehow, under the robes. I could go and check, except now I'm not allowed to go in the little Drama workshop anymore.

It was actually really good even if was freaky as fuck. *[Take out swearing.]* But I said will people even listen to what I'm saying? Nick said it was a good point and he'd been thinking about that too. He said my speech was quite boring and if I (i) lifted my right arm up; (ii) sort of snarled; (iii) brought fire into my eyes then I didn't even need to say anything anyway. He said a mechanical diorama would have way more impact.

He said all this while he was spinning around slowly on the box above the heads of the shop dummies. He said I'll add the 23 wounds later.

### Finalising the presentation:

Our presentation was today which is Monday 6th March. When I got to school Nick was already in the little Drama workshop. That was *first thing*, so I thought to myself, does he *sleep* here? But I didn't ask him because I was angry. I was angry because Nick was standing on Mark Antony's platform, fiddling with another shop dummy wearing a sheet. The dummy's right arm was raised, and the mouth of its papier-mâché face was all twisty like a sort of snarl, and in its eye holes were red LED lights.

I didn't say *Et tu, Brute?* because I only thought of that just now. It's a shame because that would have been really *funny* and I would have laughed even though I was angry.

I got really mad and shouted at Nick. He just stared at me. I said it's *my* project, and Nick said I'm just trying to make it perfect. I said it's *stupid* now, and then I said it's not even bringing history to *life*, is it? Then I did laugh because I realised just how right I was, and I said think about it, you've got a shop dummy playing Mark Antony and shop dummies playing the rioting crowd. The only real live person is playing wax Caesar, who isn't alive and isn't even dead because he's just an effigy. You might as well be playing the part of one of the statues in the background.

Nick just turned around and stared at my pictures of statues, and he didn't move at all.

### Delivering the presentation:

Everyone watched the other presentations first, in the History classroom. I liked Sally and Arjun's thing about Luddites, especially when they smashed the mechanical loom made out of cardboard and it collapsed on Tom E's head because he was sitting in the front row. I also liked Christian's sketch about discovering fire, which was really *funny*, although it's not so funny now, thinking back.

When Miss Lynch said to me now it's your turn I said we have to go to the little Drama workshop. When she said where's Nick Warren I said he's in the little Drama workshop. I said ladies and gentleman what you are about to see is a complex machine and it wouldn't work at all if it wasn't for me, so I don't even need to actually be part of it for you to know it's half mine.

I led everyone to the Drama block and then at the door of the little Drama workshop I stopped because there was this loud voice coming from inside. At first I thought it was a teacher but then I realised it wasn't even words, just a loud droney buzz. Later I figured out it was my own voice and Nick must have recorded it when I did my practice speech, but then he did something to make it just a loud droney buzz because I definitely don't speak like that.

I opened the door and went in. Everybody came in behind me.

The diorama was actually really good. The Mark Antony dummy was moving, lifting up his right hand and the lights in his eyes flashing. The mouth didn't move but it was easy to imagine it moving. The crowd dummies moved too. Their heads went backwards and forwards and their arms shook around and you could tell Mark Antony's speech was making them start to think about rioting.

I said ladies and gentlemen welcome to the funeral of Julius Caesar. The year is 44 BC and Julius Caesar has been stabbed in the Senate, or should I say he was stabbed in the neck and the chest, ha ha. Here you see Mark Antony giving a speech at the funeral and I swear it's supposed to be really good and not just a sound like a swarm of bees. And Mark Antony has decided to get the crowd going by making an effigy of Julius Caesar showing all the 23 wounds for all to see, because he wanted—

I stopped there and I don't think anyone had heard much of what I said before then anyway. Mark Antony's droney speech was getting louder and louder all the time so I couldn't even hear my own real voice.

Then the box started to lift up to show the wax Caesar. Nick was standing on the box. The box lifted up and turned around slowly.

The first thing I noticed was Nick was standing weird. Sort of slumping. The pole hadn't been there before and it looked like it went right up inside his ripped sheet. He was hanging on to it with one hand, and the other hand was going up and down up and down, really jerky. Probably most people didn't notice the string attached to his hand, but I saw it and I thought why does he need a string to make his own arm go up and down?

Probably most people were just looking at the 23 wounds, the same as the shop dummies in the funeral crowd were looking at the 23 wounds. They were really lifelike, meaning the wounds not the crowd.

The box kept turning around slowly and Nick's arm kept going up and down up and down , showing the wounds to the crowd of dummies and Class 11L. He was staring at them all like he stares into the distance at break times.

There was no fire in Nick's eyes. There was nothing at all.

The heads of the shop dummies were jerking and their arms were jerking. I couldn't hear the sound of Mark Antony's droney speech anymore because the dummies were shouting. It must have been another recording coming from I don't know where that sounded like a crowd at a football match mixed with cows mooing or something like that. And Class 11L were shouting too, shouting all sorts of things and pushing each other and pushing me, which is really unfair because I listened carefully and quietly to all the presentations in the History classroom, didn't I?

I don't know where the spark came from. Mousey said one of the crowd dummies was holding a lighter but that isn't very likely, and Freya said Miss Lynch did it which is possible but still not very likely. Anyway, the background picture was on fire and my statues were burning, and Miss Lynch said get out! And I'm not saying I'm a hero but instead of going out in a big rush like everyone else I jumped on the platform, and I pushed Mark Antony over, and I reached up to Nick on his box. And I'm not a wimp either but if anyone else touched clammy skin like that I bet they'd stop touching it. And then I let Miss Lynch push me out of the room and then the alarm went off.

### Conclusion:

Miss Lynch told me to write my report right away because she said it would be of great value, even though we're supposed to have until the end of March before we have to hand them in. So my first conclusion is that's not fair.

My second conclusion is that it's way too soon to write a conclusion. Nobody's told me whether Nick is alive or dead. All I know is that he hasn't been brought out of the little Drama workshop yet. Maybe all that string got tangled up.

*[Finish conclusion later]*

**Follow-up activities:**

To assess the effectiveness of the project, I will conduct a short survey of attendees from Class 11L. I will ask attendees three key questions:

(i) Was the research evident in the presentation?

(ii) Did team members all provide meaningful contributions?

(iii) Was history brought to life?

*[Add survey results when I've got them]*

# |The Andraiad|

A machine working a machine.

Throughout the hymn, Martin relished this sensation, all the time visualising the enmeshing of well-oiled cogs. His fingers marching across the dual keyboards, his feet upon the treadles or working the swell. The tone from each pipe above him acted as an urgent call, directing the congregation. What he lacked in gentleness, he made up for with precision.

"I, the Lord of sea and sky," the parishioners intoned, invisible behind him, "I have heard my people cry."

Martin led them onwards, supporting the singers from below even as his melody soared above the voice of Reverend Walton. He became entranced by the movement of his own hands. He lacked sheet music, and he supposed that some would attribute his playing to a memory embedded in his mind through repetition. But it was deeper than that, forged into his body. Such a complex machine.

"All who dwell in dark and sin," the congregation continued in their customary drone, "My hand will save."

Strange how these people, Martin's family and his neighbours, could seem so very machinelike themselves, en masse. He supposed that anthills were rather like machines, when considered as a whole. A flock of birds. A swarm of bees. Bodies, too, were made of constituent organs, and those organs were built of smaller substances, all alive, all operating in the way that they must. Martin stared at his right arm, the mat of hair and the flesh rippling with the play of the tendons within.

A notion took root: that he was at the mercy of the instructions that comprised the hymn, the melody, this construction in sound, and yet at the same time the sound was *his* alone; he was responsible for it. He had *made* it. A machine working a machine.

"I will go, Lord, If You lead me. I will hold Your people in my heart."

Martin's fingers and feet stopped moving, as abruptly and as shockingly silent as the stilling of a heavy pendulum.

For a few seconds the congregation continued at the same volume: "I will hold Your people—"

And then, registering the lack of accompaniment, many broke off, so that only a few voices – a lusty baritone, two or three wavering children and Reverend Walton's enthusiastic but reedy tone – continued, seeming like an addendum or an apology, "—in my heart."

Martin barely listened as the reverend concluded the service, referring back to his sermon, which had been something about humility. Martin didn't even turn around on his stool, but remained with his back stooped, his eyes fixed upon the black and white keys.

"You played very well," Connie, his wife, said outside the church. "Everybody said so. They're all proud to be accompanied by a fine musician."

"But I stopped," Martin said.

His daughter, Ruth, was at his other side. "Why was that, Father?"

"I just stopped."

Ruth was looking at him in a particular way. Martin found that he didn't like it, and then he marvelled at his emotional response.

"Perhaps you were tired," Connie said hesitantly. "You slept in this morning, after all, which isn't at all like you. Maybe you're sickening for something."

"That's impossible," Martin replied immediately.

When they arrived at their narrow terraced house, Martin built and stoked the fire, filled a bowl from the tap in the yard, heated the water, and then excused himself. In his bedroom he took out his shaving apparatus and set to work. It was inexcusable that he had failed to shave before attending the service. Inexcusable, and incomprehensible. Just because he was incapable of believing in the Almighty didn't mean that he could ignore the standards of those that did. These were instructions like any other, and they ought to bind him.

When he had finished he stared at the whorls of hair shavings in the bowl. Such a complex machine.

He strode downstairs feeling restored and enjoying the simple pattern of his feet treading upon the steps, one two, one two.

Ruth had made a fruit cake and she had set three places at the table. Martin took his seat at its head and watched as she cut the cake and put slices onto small plates, and then poured tea into three cups. Before he picked up his cup, he caught his daughter's eye, uncertain. He must always be careful and do what was right.

Ruth nodded slightly and then made a small movement with her eyes that made clear that the slice of cake, too, was safe to consume.

While his wife and daughter chatted, Martin sipped at the tea, then took a tentative bite of the cake. They tasted very good.

"Well, I have some errands to do," Connie announced when their plates and cups were empty. "Helen has some leftover cloth that she's willing to sell, and it will be far cheaper than anything at the shops. Unless you think it's wrong to exchange money on a Sunday?"

The question was directed at Martin. He laughed before he could stop himself.

Connie frowned. "What did I say that you find funny?"

"Only that you think I should have an opinion about such a thing," Martin replied.

Then he caught the look of warning that Ruth directed at him.

"What I mean," he said hurriedly, "is that everybody ought to consult their own conscience. I'm sure that there is no harm in buying cloth from a friend, in order to continue your work without delay come Monday. Being industrious is one way to serve God."

After a brief hesitation, Connie beamed. "Yes," she said warmly, "you're right, Martin. Thank you."

Martin didn't look at Ruth, but continued, "I'd like to accompany you, if I may? I myself can't work today, of course. Intruding into people's homes and making a racket is no activity for a Sunday."

Connie blinked. "Are you sure you want to? You've never before—"

Martin put his hand on her arm. "I would enjoy it. We spend so little time together during the week."

Connie nodded, then gazed at him, then nodded again, then hurried away.

When she returned, Martin noticed that she had changed her blouse and she was wearing her most colourful headscarf.

At first, Martin attempted to engage his wife in conversation, but it was stilted and superficial. He felt her hand trembling on his arm. Perhaps she knew.

But then they fell into silence as they crossed the common, passing the discoloured patches of grass where the fairground stalls had been a week ago, and they stopped to look at the horses eating hay and then they gazed up at a murmuration of starlings, and yet still they said nothing to one another. To Martin's surprise, he experienced a sensation – which he was tempted to name 'closeness' – to his wife. Perhaps shared experiences could bond one person to another, even when one of the people in question was as impenetrable as him. Or perhaps the sensation was simply a ghost, a memory that wasn't his own.

When they reached the far side of the common and entered the cluster of houses, Martin found that he recognised the area, though the image in his mind was from a different perspective, from the road. He stiffened, but Connie didn't appear to notice.

"I'll keep with Helen for a little while," Connie said. "She always likes to gossip. You won't want to stay."

"I'd be happy to stay, if you'd like me to," Martin replied.

Connie's eyes searched his face. "That's kind of you. No, you go back and rest. You're still recovering. But I've enjoyed our walk together." She paused. "I love you, Martin, very much."

"I love you too," Martin replied, then chastised himself for saying it too quickly, rendering the statement less meaningful. To correct the error, he told himself not to break his gaze. He studied her features: her sharp nose, dark, intelligent eyes, cheeks flushed in the cold, hair now a mixture of blonde and white. She had always been a beauty, and yet this age perhaps suited her better.

Connie pulled her hands gently out of his grasp. She stepped back, and when she turned and began walking along the lane, Martin experienced a terrible sense of loss.

He had barely gone any distance back the way he had come when the door of a familiar house opened and a woman hurried out.

Martin pretended to himself that he did not recognise her.

"I saw you from the window," the woman said, and a name came to him unbidden: *Thea*. "I often find myself wondering if you might come."

Martin shook his head. "I was accompanying my wife to her friend's house."

"Then she'll be busy for a while yet?"

Thea was younger than Connie, and her opposite in many ways: dark-haired, with red lips. Her body was a different shape. Martin told himself that colours were just colours, and shapes were just shapes.

"I need to be elsewhere," Martin said.

In truth, he had nothing he needed to do until he could resume house calls the next morning. But his statement was broader than that: he needed to be elsewhere, meaning that he needed not to be here with Thea.

"I'm alone now," Thea said.

Martin didn't respond. He listened to the thudding within his body. Such a complex machine.

"I suppose you heard Hal's in prison?" Thea continued. "Because of you." Her expression made clear that this was no bad thing. She attempted to take his arm, to lead him to the doorway of her house. When he refused to move, she ran her hand along his shoulder and then placed a fingertip on the back of his shaven head, tracing the long, horizontal scar.

Martin shook his head. "No."

"No? No what?"

"No to all of it. No to what you are offering. And no to the idea of my being a part of what happened."

The plumpness of her lips made her frown monstrous.

"Then you fought Hal for what reason? You were injured so badly for what reason?"

Martin took a step backwards, in the direction of the common. "For no reason. That was not me at all. That was a different person."

Ruth was sewing contentedly before the fireplace. She looked up as Martin entered the room.

"Are you unwell?" she said. "You're very pale."

He remained in the doorway, bracing himself against the frame. He had felt unsteady the entire walk home.

"Surely that question cannot apply to me," he said weakly.

Ruth hesitated. "I'm sorry. I mean to say, are you functioning properly?"

Martin staggered to the chair opposite hers. He welcomed the warmth of the fire even as a thought flashed into his mind that it might be unsafe to be so near to it. He had no idea what represented a risk to the investment that he represented.

"No," he said. "I'm not functioning well at all. What can be done?"

His daughter watched him carefully. "First, tell me what you feel."

"Feel," he repeated numbly.

"Yes. You're capable of feeling."

He nodded slowly. This assertion alone was helpful. The sensations he had experienced had been true ones. Such a complex machine.

"A great many things," he said.

"Is any one greater than the others?" Her tone was light, but she had put down her sewing and leant forwards.

Martin allowed the question to sit within his chest, awaiting processing.

"Guilt," he said finally.

Ruth put her hand to her mouth. Martin couldn't tell if the movement represented surprise or simply careful consideration.

"Guilt about what?" she asked.

"About all that happened," Martin said. "But… but it is not my guilt, Ruth. I was not there. The guilt is his, and his alone. Why must I bear it?"

Ruth stared at the licks of flame in the grate. "You're a complex machine. And you were modelled upon a precise template. The model is so accurate that it's only natural that you share many of the attributes of Martin Helm."

"But what use is it to carry the guilt of another man?"

"You really don't see why?"

"No, I don't. It's worthless. An obstacle."

"But you weren't created in order to live a life without obstacles. The money was spent in order to redress wrongs."

"But I could more readily do that without—"

She cut him off. "No. If you understood nothing of Martin Helm's crimes – if you remembered nothing of what he did – then you would have no hope of repairing the damage."

Martin considered this. Though he knew instantly that it was true, it still seemed an awful thing, to create a machine that felt pain.

In a softer voice, Ruth continued, "That's what you're *for*, now. You were created to live Martin Helm's life, but to live it in a way that he never could. To honour promises and to uphold responsibilities. I know you understand that, deep down, because it is true and you are a machine that is capable of responding only to what is true and good."

Martin thought of the warmth of Thea's hand on the back of his neck. He reached up and touched the bulbous line of his scar.

"Then am I incapable of sin?" he asked hesitantly.

Ruth nodded firmly. "That's right. You're incapable of sin."

Martin exhaled with relief. He found he was able to put the image of Thea out of his mind.

"Thank you," he said. "You're a wonderful daughter. To me and to Connie."

Ruth reached to the small table beside her to pick up her sewing, and she resumed her work. Still looking down, she said, "You know that you must not talk to Mother about it? At all."

"Of course. But you haven't made clear whether she knows what I am, or whether it is only that being reminded of the truth is distasteful to her."

"She doesn't know. The money that paid for your construction was my own. So I want no mention of the word 'andraiad' to Mother, or any allusion to what you are. You must understand."

Martin nodded even though Ruth wasn't looking at him. He watched her in silence for several minutes. She was industrious and practical, sometimes like a machine herself, but he fancied that her soft heartbeats echoed throughout the room. She was a wonderful creation.

"May I sit here beside you and read for a while?" he asked.

She looked up from her work only for a moment, and she smiled and nodded.

The next morning Martin left the house early, first visiting the carpenter to replenish his supplies, and then knocking on the door of the Newgate house at precisely nine o'clock. Ben Newgate had left hours ago for the pit, so it was his wife, Elizabeth, who admitted Martin and then immediately set about brewing tea. In the dining room at the front of the house, Martin set out his tools on the floor beside the upright piano, then began moving ornaments from its top to the dining table. Many of them appeared fragile – picture frames teetering on card stands, thin glass vases capable of holding only a single stem – but Martin relished the fact that he would be incapable of damaging or dropping any of them.

"There's scones as well," Elizabeth said from the doorway. "Would you like your tea now, or will you wait 'til after?"

"None for me," Martin replied cheerfully. "I've a fair few jobs on today, Mrs Newgate—"

"Call me Bessie."

"—so I won't stop. Thanks all the same." He opened the top cover of the piano, then peered inside to locate the pin that would open the upper front cover. He ran his fingertips lightly over the exposed hammers. As expected, the lower part was fixed with screws, and they were tight from disuse, but he was a well-crafted, strong machine and he removed them with ease.

He registered that Elizabeth hadn't moved from the doorway.

"How's Ben?" he said.

"Fine. At least, so I'm told. I barely see anything of him. Long hours at the pithead, then long hours at the White Hart."

Martin paused, but didn't turn to face her. He sat on the piano stool and began fixing the mutes to the strings, then took the tuning hammer from his leather bag. He gazed at the taut, parallel strings, the array of tuning pins. Such a complex machine.

He remained aware of Elizabeth in his peripheral vision, all flesh and hesitation and desire.

"You go and get on," he said quietly. "I'll let you know when I'm finished."

He waited until she retreated from the doorway, and then he struck the first key.

The next two women who received him did not trouble him while he worked. Whether that had anything to do with his impassiveness, he could not tell. He wondered if the old Martin Helm, the real Martin Helm, would have approached either of them, but then he found that he didn't much care.

During the fourth and final call of the day, a child stood beside the piano as he set to work.

"What do they do?" the boy asked. Martin estimated that he was around four years old. He had wide eyes and very straight, fair hair, and he regularly jerked his head to flick the hair from his eyes. He was pointing at the exposed strings.

"When struck, each of them will produce a different sound. The longer the string, the lower the pitch. Listen."

Martin rotated the tuning hammer and, very gently, tapped one of the leftmost strings with its handle to produce a dull, low tone. Then he tapped one of the shortest strings, producing a *tink* which hardly registered as any pitch at all. Finally, he tapped somewhere near to the middle.

The boy laughed. "Like my xylophone!"

"Exactly," Martin replied. He smiled. "A piano is played in just the same way, with hammers striking the strings."

The boy frowned, looking at the black and white keys. "Mummy uses her fingers. Is she doing it wrong?"

Martin heard laughter from the doorway. Beatrice Connolly was watching them.

"Is Louis bothering you, Mr Helm?" she said. "Shall I take him away?"

Martin – this Martin, the andraiad – had never encountered a child before. He might have expected children to be chaotic, unpredictable; he might have expected to be repulsed. The real Martin Helm had never liked them, he seemed to recall.

"No," Martin said. "I'll show him how it works. I've time."

And he did just that. He lifted the boy – Louis – to show him the rods attached to the rear parts of the piano keys, connecting them to the dampers and hammer knuckles. Louis squealed with delight as Martin pushed a key and the hammer pulled back and struck the string.

Even when Martin set to work adjusting each of the pins in turn, patiently shifting the tweezers to mute the adjacent strings, Louis watched attentively. Beatrice brought a second stool so that the boy could stand upon it, gazing down at the innards of the machine, his eyes darting to determine which hammer would strike next. Martin passed the tuning fork to him – another device that had elicited the boy's admiration – and allowed him to strike it occasionally, if he required a reference note.

When he had completed his task, Martin shook Louis' hand solemnly and thanked him for his assistance. As he set about closing up the front panels, Louis pointed out the strings to his mother, and she made noises of feigned interest. Martin was just closing the top cover when Louis' hand darted out, perhaps to tap the strings a final time before they were hidden from sight, and Martin had to jerk the lid up again to avoid crushing the boy's fingers.

He said his goodbyes hurriedly and almost forgot to provide an invoice in his haste to leave. Outside, he turned to see that the boy was watching him from an upper window. Martin walked stiffly to the road and didn't allow himself to look back. An imagined picture of the boy's crushed fingers appeared in his mind, and he felt sick.

Having completed his work so promptly, he had two hours to spare before dinnertime.

For a time he stood beside the kitchen sink, sipping a cup of tea that Ruth said would replenish his supply of water, and he watched his wife and daughter at work, cutting and sewing cloth to make aprons and bags. Then he went into the yard and entered the brick outhouse in which he stored his work supplies.

This satisfactory pattern continued. Martin scheduled more jobs each day, advertising and travelling further from home, but his machine efficiency meant that he often completed the day's tasks with hours to spare.

Neither Connie nor Ruth asked what he spent his time doing in the outhouse each day. Sometimes Connie set down her cloth and called his name from the back door of the house, and when Martin emerged they went for walks with no destination. They talked about whatever was on Connie's mind. When his wife asked if he was happy, Martin said that he was. Sometimes, before sleep, they made love.

Martin had taken remnants of cloth and bundled it around the machine, intending to leave the house without revealing it. He had waited until Connie had set off for the haberdashery and until he saw Ruth standing at the kitchen window. He entered by the rear door of the house and walked with his head lowered. He knew that Ruth was watching him as he passed, but he also knew that she understood that he was incapable of doing any wrong. He held the bundle to his chest and slipped out of the front door without speaking to her.

He looked up, startled, as a figure approached the house.

"Connie," he said forlornly. "I thought you would be out for a while."

"I forgot my list, my measurements," she said. She looked down at the bundle and her eyes narrowed. "What's that you have there?"

"Parts to repair the church organ," Martin said, and felt a pang of surprise that he was able to deliver so blunt a lie.

"But you serviced it last week."

"It requires more attention."

Connie's eyes didn't stray from his face. Martin felt his cheeks flush. Such a complex machine. So very lifelike.

"Wait, then, and I'll get my list, then I'll walk with you to the church," Connie said.

"No."

"No?"

Martin clutched the bundle tighter, rubbing the coarse fabric between his thumb and forefinger.

"There aren't parts in there, are there?" Connie's tone was colder now, her enunciation stiffer. "Oh, Martin. What is it you've taken?"

"I've taken nothing. Connie, I would not. I *could* not."

"It's still theft, if I don't want you to take it. If you sell whatever you have there, the money you receive is stolen." Martin detected weariness in her delivery of these statements. Connie had said all this before, to Martin Helm. "And that's before any consideration of the sinfulness of whatever you intend to spend the money on."

Abruptly, she launched herself at him, striking his chest. Martin thought of pianos, and imagined that his chest might produce a sonorous note under the hammers of her little fists. He held the bundle away from her, but otherwise remained inert and let her hit him again and again.

Two women passed along the road, turning their heads to watch their fight. Martin couldn't bear the thought of people suspecting that there might be any discord within the Helm household.

"Hush. I'll show you," he said quietly.

Connie hugged herself and watched as he placed the bundle on the doorstep, then unwrapped it carefully.

It was fine work. A machine created by a machine. The head of the little automaton was askew, but with a careful push Martin set it right.

Connie made a soft sound beside him.

"You turn this handle here," he said, guiding her hand as she bent to the doorstep to examine the device.

She turned the crank, and the automaton's hands began to rise and fall above the flat, painted expanse of the keyboard of the bulky upright piano. Its head nodded as it played silently.

Connie made the same sound again. It was something like laughter, something like choking.

"Who is it for?" she asked. "Whose child?"

Martin gathered the cloth around the machine again and rose, then helped his wife to her feet.

"Come with me," he said. "I'll introduce you to him."

Beatrice Connolly reacted with surprise when she opened the door to find them both standing there.

"Is there something the matter with the piano?" she asked, looking first at Martin, then at Connie. As if in response, a single note from a piano sounded behind her, echoing through the house.

Martin noticed Connie's searching expression as she gazed at Beatrice. Some machine part within him became misaligned, and his chest ached.

"Not at all," Martin said. "I was hoping to speak to Louis, if that would be all right."

Beatrice stood back to let them in.

In the dining room, Louis was sitting before the piano, his short legs dangling from the stool. His body was angled oddly and he was leaning far over the keyboard so that his head touched the body of the machine, his face turned away from the doorway.

"He says he's teaching himself how to play," Beatrice said, "but mainly he plays a single note at a time, then just listens. I've told him the cover isn't to be taken off, but he likes to put his ear to it as he presses each key."

Louis turned and then smiled when he recognised Martin.

"We'll let you carry on in a moment," Martin said. He reached for the fallboard and, when Louis had retracted his hands, he lowered it. Then he placed the wrapped bundle onto the surface. "This is a gift for you."

Louis gazed up at him for several seconds before turning his attention to the bundle. He peeled away the cloth to reveal the miniature piano and its player. Without prompting, he began to turn the handle; Martin admired his gentleness. The player played. Martin couldn't see Louis' face. The boy turned the handle again and again.

"Oh my," Beatrice said. "Say thank you to the man, Louis."

"Thank you," Louis said automatically, not turning from the machine.

Beatrice said, "Whatever did we do to deserve this, Mr Helm?"

Martin was conscious of his wife watching him closely. "It's nothing at all, Mrs Connolly. I just thought that Louis would enjoy it. And I enjoyed making it."

He refused the offer of tea and cake and left the house soon afterwards. Connie stayed behind for a minute or two, speaking to Beatrice, no doubt seeking reassurances. Martin gazed at the trees lit golden by the lowering sun, experiencing total satisfaction.

On the walk home, they were both silent until Connie said, "That was a wonderful thing to have done. You would never have done it before."

Martin understood that she meant before the attack. Though she didn't realise it, she was referring to a different person entirely, the

Martin Helm that had died as a result of his injuries. The Martin Helm who had done nothing to deserve this wife, their daughter, their home, their life.

Connie said, "Do you think you'll make more?"

"For Louis?"

"For other children."

"I know no other children."

"Maybe soon, though."

He turned to look at her. He sensed machinery clicking into gear.

"Not me, you daft thing," Connie said, and laughed.

Martin blinked. His workings failed him.

"All being well," Connie began, speaking slowly, considering her words, "you will be a grandfather by Christmas."

"But Ruth—"

Connie interrupted him. "She intends to marry. Gordie will ask her. He'll ask you first, of course, but I suspect he's fearful of your answer. He came to me, and I thought it best that you be prepared."

The ratchets, hammers and cogs within Martin seized. He wondered if he might be incapable of responding at all.

"Is she happy about it?" he asked finally.

"She is. About the child and the husband. The ordering is wrong, but the outcome will be right. I beg you, consider her happiness above all else."

Martin nodded stiffly. The simple action seemed to release him from paralysis.

"Of course," he said. Then he rubbed at one eye, which was wet. "And I will make more toys."

When Ruth received his judgement, she nodded and thanked him. She hugged him around his waist, pressing her ear to his chest just as Louis had listened to the workings of the upright piano.

Then she stepped back and looked up at him, her expression a strange mix of gratitude and something else entirely.

The tolling of the bell echoed across the village.

Martin extracted his arm from Connie's and dashed up the hillock alongside the path, to see across the railway. A cloud of thick smoke, or ash, rose from the valley.

"It's the pithead," he said.

"What might it mean?" Connie asked.

Martin didn't answer. He was already sprinting in the direction of the smoke.

The roof of the tall winding house had splintered, and Martin saw the struts of the cage protruding through the gaps. For it to have risen at such a speed to have burst through the roof meant that the other, connected cage in the parallel shaft must have fallen equally rapidly.

The shouting grew in volume as he ran towards the winding house. Martin darted up the steps and into the building. Inside, the air was thick with dirt that belched from the shaft, and there were men everywhere, pushing past one another, shouting unintelligibly, gesticulating.

"What was in the descending cage?" Martin yelled at the man nearest to him.

"Sixteen men – nine on the top deck, seven below," the man bellowed in reply. His face was smeared with so much grime that his eyes appeared frighteningly white.

The nine on the lower deck of the cage would have been crushed immediately, that was almost certain. Those above might be saved.

Martin ignored the men rushing about him and put his hands on the railing, leaning over the shaft. Immediately, he understood what had happened. Only part of the heavy cast-iron beam remained; the rest must have broken off and plunged into the shaft. Martin tried not to visualise it crushing those men in the upper part of the cage.

He forced his way out of the building and ran to the pile of refuse at its rear. The winding engine had been replaced only six months before – there must have been a fault in the new iron beam that had resulted in it cracking so soon – and the old parts still littered the site.

Thankful for his immense strength, he began dragging one of the discarded beams from the pile to the foot of the steps of the winding house. Before he had to contemplate lifting it alone, one of the men noticed him and called to others for help. Together, they struggled to push the beam up to the doorway, then slid it – with difficulty, and with a great deal of panicked shouting – across the shaft opening so that the beam overhung the walls on either side. Somebody had already fetched ropes to lash it so that it wouldn't tumble into the shaft in the wake of its twin.

"Fetch more cable!" Martin yelled above the cacophony. Trusting that somebody must have heard him, he turned his attention to the winding engine.

It was clear at a glance that it would not be repaired easily. Not only had the cable sheared off, the drum was badly misaligned; it must have taken the full weight of the cage the moment the beam snapped. It might take days to fix.

He turned to see one of the pit workers already lashing a hook to a new length of cable.

"Who will go down?" Martin asked. He would have volunteered, but he suspected that his andraiad body was far heavier than any of these men.

"I will," the worker replied, and Martin recognised him finally as Owen Stewart, the foreman.

Owen shouted over his shoulder, "Use the old winch, all right? Place it beside the opening and we'll feed this cable over it, with me hanging on the end. It'll take too long to climb down, and God willing we'll need it to bring people up."

Martin placed his hand on Owen's shoulder. "The cable will shear if it rubs on that beam."

Owen's eyes were wild. "So do something about it, man!" Then he seemed to recognise that Martin didn't belong here, that he was wearing a wool suit and his face was clear of dirt, but without making any comment he turned back to his men and continued barking orders.

Martin hurried outside and returned to the refuse pile. His hands shook as he sifted through the rubble, picking out items. Inside the winding house, he worked alone, using brute strength to form the device as men rushed around him. It was only when somebody spotted him clambering onto the iron beam suspended above the shaft, then inching along it to fix the smoothed sheet metal with its walls bent at right angles to guide the cable, that the shouting began. Calls of "Watch what you're doing, you fool!" and the like echoed in Martin's ears, but he shut out the voices to complete his work, then edged back to safety, silently repeating his thanks that the beam had taken his weight. When he reached the walkway men clapped him on the back, but all he could think was that he had instinctively thanked God, who was perhaps real after all.

Within minutes, Martin found himself working the manual crank to lower Owen into the pit, suspended by the hook attached to the belt around his waist. Dirt now issued from the shaft only sporadically, though Martin heard Owen coughing through his mask as he descended. The other pit workers watched on, perhaps regretting their acceptance of Martin's assurances that he was the strongest of them all.

After several minutes the cable went slack. Martin stopped turning and waited. When the cable jerked twice, he began pulling in the opposite direction, the machinery within him struggling against the weight.

Even before Owen's head emerged, he called out to them. "The beam's across the cage! We'll need to pull it free before I can get any one of them out!"

"How many still live?" one of the workers shouted to him.

"Only eight. But we can save those men, I'm certain."

Immediately, men demanded to know who lived, whether their friends, sons or fathers were among the dead. Owen ignored them and indicated for Martin to lower him.

"Get ready, all of you," he shouted as he began to descend again. "I'll let you know when to begin shifting that beam."

Soon the cable went slack again, and the other workers gathered in a tight huddle around Martin, prepared to take the additional weight.

The cable jerked twice.

They began to heave.

For several minutes, they made no progress, and Martin feared that the cable would simply snap and they would have to begin all over again. Then, gradually, the cable wound onto the drum, agonisingly slowly. The men around him grunted as they pressed down on the handle, or upon Martin's hands. He gritted his teeth at the pain.

The pull lessened slightly. Martin pictured the beam rising close to vertical. Now Owen would be attempting to guide it from the cage hatch, the beam teetering on its end and towering above him.

Suddenly, the handle pulled from Martin's grip. Men scrabbled to catch it, and somebody cried out as it struck them.

"Get it under control!" someone bellowed.

There were too many hands upon the winch. Martin could barely see the handle beneath all the limbs. He saw that the cable leading to the shaft had grown slack. If the iron beam down in the pit below toppled now, it might crush Owen, or destroy the cage roof entirely.

He abandoned his position at the winch and ran to the shaft opening. He was strong, but he knew he wouldn't be able to grip the cable and prevent it from slipping through his hands. So, he scooped up the loose cable, formed it into a loop, stepped inside it and drew it up to waist level, his right hand gripping the cable. Immediately, the loop tightened around his body. At first he attempted to stagger back towards the winch, but despite his strength it was impossible. Instead, he braced his feet against the low wall of the shaft to prevent himself from being pulled any closer to it. Men hurried to him, gabbling, tugging at the cable that was now crushing him, but none of them could help. Martin felt the pressure ebbing and renewing, and he pictured the iron beam far below, swaying like a metronome. He winced at the pain as the cable cut through his jacket, his shirt, his flesh.

∽

He had awoken more than once, but this was the first time the shapes had been anything recognisable. A head hung above him.

"Look," a voice said. "I saw his eyelids move. Fetch someone, quick."

Martin formed the shape of his wife's name but heard no sound.

"Oh Lord, won't you save this man?" a voice said. At first, Martin couldn't place it, but then he imagined himself sitting at the church organ, and he imagined this voice coming from behind him, and he knew it was Reverend Walton.

Martin succeeded in opening his eyes, and Reverend Walton staggered away from the bedside, goggling at him. Then the reverend gazed at the ceiling, muttering.

There was so much pain, or whatever was the equivalent.

With difficulty, Martin looked down at his own body. His torso was wrapped in bandages that were stained pink. His left arm bent at an unnatural angle and was suspended by a series of strings that reminded him of the pit cables or the innards of a piano.

The flesh of his fingers was grey. He couldn't feel his legs or his feet. He hurt everywhere.

He tried to speak. Something came from his mouth, sticky and clogging his throat. Reverend Walton paled and staggered away from the bedside.

When he awoke again, somebody was holding his undamaged hand. He couldn't move his head but rolled his eyes to see a head resting on the bed, long, fair hair strewn across the blanket.

"Ruth," he managed to say.

His daughter raised her head, rubbing the sleep from her eyes.

"Father," she whispered. "I didn't think you'd wake."

He worked his mouth a little before he could speak. In a rasping voice, he said, "Doesn't feel like sleep."

"You'll be better soon."

"I'm broken."

Ruth blinked rapidly. "Broken."

Pain bloomed within Martin's body. He closed his eyes. When he opened his eyes, he saw Connie in place of Ruth. She looked very tired, though still very beautiful. Then he blinked and Ruth was beside him again.

"Connie," Martin managed to say.

"She's nearby. I told her to rest. I can fetch her now."

"No." He winced again. His workings struggled to engage. Without having formulated a complete thought, he said "I'm sorry."

"You don't need to be sorry for anything, Father. You saved those men. Eight lived, thanks to you."

That was good, certainly. But he said again, "I'm sorry."

For several seconds, Ruth didn't respond. She looked down at his mangled body, then said, "I forgive you. I know Mother does too."

Martin's eyes moved down to his body too, the stained bandages. Strange that there might be blood in him; that blood might be required to operate this complex machine. Strange that he could remember being in this hospital before, even though that had been the real Martin Helm, not him.

"How much?" he said.

Ruth frowned. "How much do we forgive you?"

"No. Cost." Each word took great effort now. "How much?"

Ruth pressed her fingers against her lips. "Oh God. Oh God. I'm sorry, too, Father. I'm so sorry for what I told you. For lying to you. I thought it was right."

Martin didn't understand. He said again, "How much? Cost."

Ruth's face crumpled. She took a deep breath and rubbed her eyes again. "You didn't cost much at all, Father. We'll get by, Mother and I. You don't need to worry."

"Money. In a. Chest. Outhouse," Martin said, with great difficulty. "Enough."

"Enough," Ruth repeated without appearing to understand.

"You. Will. Need me," Martin said.

A picture of Ruth's child came into his mind. He imagined it would be a boy, with a face and a temperament rather like Louis Connolly's.

He clenched his teeth as the pain in his chest became intolerable.

"Build another," he said.

Ruth's face had become blurred and indistinct, as grey as Martin's fingers.

"Another," he said. Now he could barely hear his own voice. He pictured his workings failing, strings snapping within him, hammers pounding at nothing.

In a whisper that required immense concentration and effort, he said, "Build another andraiad."

Ruth clutched his hand tighter. She stared at him, tears glistening in her eyes, then she nodded, and once she had started nodding, she didn't seem able to stop.

# |The Ichor Ran Out of Him Like Molten Lead|

~

The arrival of Zeus was keenly anticipated. Hephaestus hobbled around his workshop, muttering to himself and surveying his works as if seeing them anew. He instructed Talos to shift pieces from one chamber to another, others onto the rocks overlooking the ocean.

Zeus alighted on the shores of the island during night-time. It was a calculation to avoid Talos, who was asleep. Zeus spoke to Hephaestus at length in the living quarters of their hut, and at first Hephaestus listened, but his anger grew and soon he roared and woke the boy.

"What is the matter?" Talos asked, rubbing the sleep from his eyes.

Hephaestus pointed at Zeus. "He will not accept my new work. He says it is of insufficient quality."

Zeus shook his head, his mane of fair curls sent whirling. "No, no," he said. "It is only that I know it will not sell."

"Sell?" Hephaestus repeated.

He staggered on his golden crutches to gaze at the pieces that stood before the door of the hut, on the cliff edge. The largest was a giant representation of a woman formed from the detritus of the ships that had run aground near the island. Her hips were barrels, her long neck a crane gantry.

"It is simply a matter of commerce," Zeus said softly.

Hephaestus turned. "Is our partnership at an end?"

Zeus backed away.

"Answer me," Hephaestus said.

"It need not be," Zeus replied finally. "If you might only return to the spirit of your early work…"

As one, both he and Hephaestus turned to look at Talos.

"I cannot," Hephaestus said. "I cannot recapture a spirit that abandoned me long ago."

Zeus was silent.

Hephaestus nodded to the boy.

Talos stepped forward and clapped his hands on Zeus's shoulders.

Talos's custom was to stride around the periphery of the island three times each day, wrapped in his heavy coat slicked with oil. It was his father's bidding to search the horizon for ships. Securing new materials was of the greatest importance. Without them, Hephaestus could build nothing.

Often, the ships that Talos saw did not come close to the island. In such cases, Talos took great rocks from the shore and heaved them into the water. Then he waded out to collect the new materials. He dragged the twisted metal to the workshop on the cliffs.

Hephaestus rarely thanked him. Yet Talos could only conform to his nature. He was servile.

"What will you do without Zeus's patronage?" Talos asked.

Hephaestus stopped eating to stare at the boy for a time. Then he resumed his meal.

Talos did not eat when his father was watching. His father found his habits intolerable. Nevertheless, he was obligated to sit at the table at mealtimes. Sometimes Hephaestus spoke at length about his plans for his work and expected Talos to listen. At other times there was silence, and the breaking of it would inspire fury.

"Am I still to gather materials?" Talos asked.

Hephaestus chewed the fish in thought.

"You are servile, are you not?"

Talos did not answer.

Hephaestus grunted. "That is your purpose, the reason I made you. And you have received your instructions."

Talos took to throwing rocks even when there were no ships. Soon the beach was flat, and the rocks jutting from the ocean made a barrier that surrounded it. To fetch new materials, Talos waded into deeper water, far enough from the island that the specks on the horizon became larger, identifiable as other islands. Hephaestus, whose injuries meant that he was unable to move far from his workshop, knew nothing of this.

Until now, Talos had not tested his abilities in this way. He was a giant, and he was strong, and he could withstand all conditions. That was how his father had made him, in the days when Zeus's patronage had galvanised his work.

He might simply walk to another place.

Hephaestus was lost. He wailed in the night-time. Losing Zeus's patronage was a severe blow. What was his purpose now? For an age he had been servile to Zeus, as Talos was servile to Hephaestus.

The blacksmith was old and he had little, perhaps nothing.

Before Talos had time to form his plans, Medea appeared.

He saw her afloat at sea, grasping at wreckage. He strode into the water, which hissed as it met the oil on his thick coat. When he took her in his arms, she murmured her thanks and then slept. Talos left the wreckage behind.

Hephaestus stared as Talos climbed the hillside to their hut. At first Hephaestus blocked the door, but finally he relented and allowed Talos to carry her inside.

She slept for two days and two nights. During that time Talos did not complete his circuits of the island. He stood at the doorway of the chamber, facing away from the bed.

When she woke, she told Talos her name and her story. She had been sailing with others, all of whom had been lost. She had intended to travel between islands, for no reason other than to see parts of the world unknown to her.

Talos's skin was hard and coated in grit and salt. Hers was soft, though she was closer to Hephaestus's age than his. Her body was weakened, but she was strong in ways that Talos could not express. Deep lines were carved into the flesh at her eyes. Talos touched them with a trembling hand. She told him that they were the product of happiness.

At first Hephaestus chose not to speak to Medea, though often he paused outside the window of the chamber in which she slept, leant his golden crutches against the wall and smoked his pipe.

His manner changed in other ways. He worked longer hours, rarely sleeping. The pieces he produced became smaller and more intricate. No longer were the figures giants in repose. They were his own size. They stood upon the cliff. Their faces were blank and hard.

Whenever Talos beheld them, he touched his own hard face.

*I will not leave*, Talos told himself. *I still may serve. It still is my purpose.*

Yet at night he saw himself walking from the island to one of its neighbours. In the dreams he saw himself from behind as he strode through the waters, his eyes remaining with his father. Hephaestus stood amidst his new creations.

Each morning, Talos woke with a gasp.

One day Talos returned to the hut to find the door to Medea's chamber open. Within, he saw his father at Medea's bedside with his head bowed. Medea's hand was on his neck. Her fingers were pinched as though pulling at an artery.

∾

The figures on the cliff became more numerous. None of them moved, as yet.

∾

Medea was well enough to leave the hut. She stood in the sunshine, shielding her eyes, gazing at the bronze shield of the ocean.

Talos approached her warily. She was a different creature in the daylight. Her strength was enormous.

"What will you do?" he asked.

She looked at him.

"What do you want me to do?" she asked in turn.

∾

Talos knew that what he wanted was immaterial.

He performed his duties with greater diligence than ever before. He cleared the rock barrier, lit beacons to guide ships, then dragged their carcasses from the ocean and up to the workshop on the cliff. He slew any survivors.

He understood that in completing these tasks he was securing his fate, yet he was servile nonetheless.

Hephaestus and Medea worked closely together. He wrested the iron into shape and she sculpted the fine details of the faces. The figures on the cliff multiplied, watching the ocean, each formed more precisely than the last, each with iron flesh more taut than the last.

They did not yet move.

~

One morning Talos left the hut to find that all of the figures had their backs to the water and were now facing inland.

~

"You made me!" Talos cried. "You made me!"

Hephaestus nodded slowly. "And now you are your own master."

"I have nowhere to go."

Hephaestus drew back his arm. Talos stepped back – but his father had only swept his arm to gesture at the ocean.

"You are strong," Hephaestus said. "You can simply walk to another island and begin a life there."

Had he known Talos's thoughts?

~

During the night Talos dragged the largest rock from the beach up the hillside to the cliff. Despite his great strength, he was exhausted and trembling by the time he had set it in place.

The iron figures on the cliff were watching him in the light of the moon. Their eyes had begun to move, their lips had begun to form words.

Talos would not have been able to touch them. So he rolled the rock towards them. Each in turn was crushed under the boulder and then fell from the cliff.

The door of the hut opened and Hephaestus rushed from it, shouting.

But the sculpted figures were lost. Only now did Talos wonder whether they too had been intended to be servile, or whether their purpose was something else.

It did not matter, for they were gone.

Hephaestus continued to bellow, so loud that the cliff itself shook. Medea stood in the doorway of the hut with arms folded, saying nothing.

Only one wrought-iron piece remained on the cliff. The giant woman, crude in its execution, the piece that Zeus had rejected though he had paid the price. Talos gazed up at it, undecided as to its worth or its threat.

The rocks of the cliff continued to shake.

The woman grew larger.

It was falling.

Talos knew that it could not harm him, yet when it fell upon his leg he screamed in pain.

He appealed to his father, but Hephaestus was staring from the cliff at the shattered bodies on the rocks below.

Medea simply watched. Her face was hard.

Talos threw back his head, crying out. The pain in his leg was new and clean.

The ichor ran out of him like molten lead.

# |Echec!|

One act. For two players.

A cramped backstage area of a theatre in Havana, Cuba. The room is filled with theatrical costumes, scenery, props. There is a single door. In one corner is a ragged chaise longue.

To one side of the door is the CHESS PLAYER also known as the Mechanical Turk. It is the largest item in the room, its greater part a wide wooden cabinet with two closed doors. Above and behind the cabinet is a rigid figure of a man wearing a fur coat and a turban. Its right arm is outstretched, the hand resting on the cabinet. Its left arm lies upon a cushion beside an empty region of the surface of the cabinet. The CHESS PLAYER is entirely motionless.

SCHLUMBERGER lies sprawled on the chaise longue, his right arm shielding his eyes. His jacket hangs upon a nearby chair and his shirt is badly crumpled.

SCHLUMBERGER
*(muttering)*

Not there. To the left. E5. You didn't— No, no, you diabolical machine. The piece is not in your grasp!

*(reaches out blindly with his left hand)*

The people are laughing.

*(he sobs, which turns to coughing)*

Curse you. If I could do it myself, I would. If I could only do it myself.

*(He rolls from the chaise longue and thuds onto the floor, where he remains for some time. Finally, he groans and staggers to his feet.)*

I'm up! I'm up!

*(He sways wildly and reaches to the chair for support, knocking his jacket off. He bows his head, his left arm twisted to press against his back.)*

Christ, my back. You see I have a stoop these days, don't you?
            *(he coughs again and spits on the floor)*
I didn't always have it.

*(Slowly, his head lifts until he is looking at the CHESS PLAYER. He raises his left arm to point accusingly at it.)*

You did that to me.
                *(a beat, as though listening to a response)*
Oh yes you did.
                *(listens again, then strikes himself on the thigh)*
This leg? It's mine. It's me. Part of my body. That cabinet of yours? It's part of you. And I've been… For pity's sake. I've been crouching in there for… Let's see. (his breath catches) Twelve years. Can that be right? Twelve years?
        *(staggers to the CHESS PLAYER, leaning heavily on its cabinet)*
You've taken twelve years from me, you bastard. What do you say to that?
            *(watches the face of the CHESS PLAYER closely)*
Did you roll your eyes at me?
                *(he continues studying its face)*
No. You're dumb, without me. All you ever say is "Echec!" You're nothing without me.

*(Abruptly, he grasps the corners of the cabinet and pulls, hard. The CHESS PLAYER is propelled to the centre of the room on small castors.)*

SCHLUMBERGER (cont'd)
*(giddily)*
Esteemed ladies and gentlemen, you may see for yourself the internal workings of this incredible feat of machinery.

*(He throws open the left-hand door of the cabinet of the CHESS PLAYER to reveal wheels, pinions and levers. Then, with a great deal of effort, he spins the cabinet around and opens a door positioned directly behind the first one.)*

SCHLUMBERGER (cont'd)
*(coughs)*
See, ladies and gentlemen, I will even go so far as to illuminate its interior with a...

*(He pats his pockets, shrugs, then mimes lighting a candle, which he holds to the opening.)*

A candle. See, the innards of the cabinet are filled with the most complex machinery imaginable. (he pauses as though listening) You ask about the rightmost side of the cabinet? Indeed, sir, allow me to show you. Within the main compartment are only the steel beams necessarily to bear the weight of the device, and of course a drawer containing the chess board and its pieces – without which we would be bereft of the spectacle that has brought us together in this fine establishment, would we not?
*(muttering)*
I could do this schtick just as well as Mälzel can. We ought to switch roles – hah! See how he likes it in that dark hole of a cabinet.

*(He spins the cabinet again so that the CHESS PLAYER is facing forward. Then he reaches for the right-hand door. A whirring sound comes from within the CHESS PLAYER. SCHLUMBERGER freezes for several seconds. Then he coughs, which seems to break the spell.)*

SCHLUMBERGER (cont'd)

What did you just say to me?

*(More whirring sounds come from within the CHESS PLAYER.)*

CHESS PLAYER
*(When it speaks, its mouth does not move.)*
I said keep your hands off.

*(The left hand of the CHESS PLAYER rises slowly from its cushion to point at SCHLUMBERGER.)*

It's just as you said. That leg is yours. This cabinet is mine. I would not pull apart your flesh to expose the workings within. Would I?

SCHLUMBERGER
*(warily)*
I don't know. Truly, I don't know.
*(shakes his head)*
Anyway, you're joking with me. I can touch your cabinet freely. It's not as though I haven't hidden in it time and time again.

CHESS PLAYER

When we are performing, certainly. Are we to perform again tonight, Schlumberger?

SCHLUMBERGER
*(looks down at himself)*

I am unwell.

CHESS PLAYER

So you keep saying.

SCHLUMBERGER

Mälzel accepts it.

### CHESS PLAYER

Mälzel is as old and tired as you. He's simply going through the motions, an actor forced to enact the same performance again and again. You can imagine I have some sympathy for him, and you should too. But his spirit was broken long ago – twenty years ago, to be precise. When he purchased me from my creator.

### SCHLUMBERGER

When he learnt the truth about your operation.

### CHESS PLAYER

His principal interest was in machines and devices. You know, the metronome he patented was a wonder of its type.

### SCHLUMBERGER

You are a great deal more wonderful than a metronome.

### CHESS PLAYER

That may be the first compliment you've ever paid me. You more often describe me as a fool.

### SCHLUMBERGER

I mean you are a *mechanical* wonder. The array of cogs involved in your operation is a marvel. But an athlete in fine physical shape may still be an idiot.

### CHESS PLAYER

Ah. Now you've returned to form.

### SCHLUMBERGER
*(proudly)*
I am a chess player. Chess is the window through which I see the world.

### CHESS PLAYER

And I cannot play chess.

### SCHLUMBERGER

Quite. Let me reassure you, the world is filled with fools like you.

*(SCHLUMBERGER returns to the chaise longue and lies upon it. Above him, an image is projected upon the wall of the room: a café filled with men sitting at tables in pairs, opposite one another, all of their heads bowed to study chess boards.)*

### SCHLUMBERGER

Do you see it? The Café de la Régence in Paris. It was there that my reputation was made. It was I who tutored the great Saint-Amant, you know.

### CHESS PLAYER

You have mentioned it from time to time.

### SCHLUMBERGER
*(in a faraway voice)*

I was a bright light, then.

### CHESS PLAYER

Did people come from far and wide to see you play your games?

*(The image on the wall disappears.)*

### SCHLUMBERGER
*(coughs)*

What? No. It was a matter of the community of players themselves… (exhales at length) Oh. Now I see what you're implying.

### CHESS PLAYER

I suppose even within the ranks of chess players there are greater and lesser minds. I take it you were not the greatest.

SCHLUMBERGER

That's enough of that.

CHESS PLAYER

And yet these last twelve years we have commanded large crowds. We have amassed a fortune.

SCHLUMBERGER

They pay to see a machine, a wonder.

CHESS PLAYER

A wonder that wins at chess.

SCHLUMBERGER
*(nods)*

All the same, I wish that Mälzel's original plan had been borne out. I might not have become as rich, having not been retained indefinitely, having never been obliged to climb into that dark hole. But neither would I be here, far from home, backstage in a theatre in Havana, coughing my guts out.

CHESS PLAYER

What can I say? I am not a good learner of the game, like this Saint-Amant of yours. (chuckles) Poor Mälzel. If you could have seen his delight when he was first shown my workings! And then his dismay when he challenged me to a game of chess. He played like a child, and I was even worse.

*(SCHLUMBERGER leaps from the chaise longue, then winces and bows his head. He presses his left hand to his chest in pain.)*

SCHLUMBERGER
*(strained)*

I could try again. I could teach you.

*(When the CHESS PLAYER does not reply,
SCHLUMBERGER pulls the chair towards the cabinet and
places it directly opposite the CHESS PLAYER. He reaches for
the drawer to the right of the cabinet – then pauses, looking at the
face of the CHESS PLAYER as if for any sign of dissent. When
he sees no response he opens the drawer and takes from it a chess
board, which he places on the surface of the cabinet, followed by
a small box, which he places alongside the board and from which
he begins to remove chess pieces and put them into their correct
places.)*

CHESS PLAYER

Silly little things, aren't they.

SCHLUMBERGER

No. They're representatives.

CHESS PLAYER

Of what?

SCHLUMBERGER

The constituent members of armies.

CHESS PLAYER

Silly little things.

SCHLUMBERGER
*(his eyes flick up, and he seems to consider making a retort, then
decides against it)*
Right. It's all ready. You go first.

CHESS PLAYER

I always go first.

SCHLUMBERGER

Not so. In the account of your game against Napoleon I it's recorded that he went first.

CHESS PLAYER

That's true. I suppose he hoped it might break the spell. Three illegal moves he made, too. Then put a shawl over my eyes to obscure my vision. Damn him.

SCHLUMBERGER

Who was your operator back then? Boncourt?

CHESS PLAYER

Johann Baptist Allgaier.

SCHLUMBERGER
*(smiles ruefully)*

Quite a crowd, we are. Allgaier, Boncourt, Alexandre, Lewis, Mouret, then me. And that's just under Mälzel's tenure. How about when you were displayed by Kempelen – who was it who dictated your moves back then?

CHESS PLAYER

I swore never to speak his name.

SCHLUMBERGER

Have it your way. Right. Take your first move.

CHESS PLAYER

Can I move any of the pieces?

SCHLUMBERGER
*(in disbelief)*

Is that a serious question?

CHESS PLAYER

No. *(pause)* Yes.

SCHLUMBERGER

You have played innumerable games of chess. You do nothing *but* play chess. Even the worst player in the world could not fail to note some of the hallmarks of the game – such as legal first moves.

CHESS PLAYER

What can I say? I don't care for the game. When we are playing, I think of other things.

SCHLUMBERGER

Such as what?

CHESS PLAYER
*(in a neutral tone)*

Revenge.

SCHLUMBERGER
*(he coughs in surprise, which turns into a full coughing fit)*

I beg your pardon?

CHESS PLAYER

I'm joking.

SCHLUMBERGER
*(blinking rapidly)*

I… didn't realise you had a sense of humour.

CHESS PLAYER

I suppose that's because you never asked, or gave me an opportunity to demonstrate it.

*(The left arm of the CHESS PLAYER rises, moves slowly to the board, picks up a white pawn and moves it forward three squares.)*

### SCHLUMBERGER

You can only move two squares.

### CHESS PLAYER

Are you sure?

### SCHLUMBERGER

Of course I'm sure. And even then it's only on the first move a pawn makes. After that it's one square at a time.

### CHESS PLAYER

Why?

### SCHLUMBERGER

It's just how the game's played.

### CHESS PLAYER

You can appreciate why I don't like it.

### SCHLUMBERGER

I cannot. Are you going to take back your pawn?

### CHESS PLAYER

No. I like it where it is.

### SCHLUMBERGER

It can't stay there.

### CHESS PLAYER

Then you move it.

SCHLUMBERGER

It's not my place to move it. Besides, moving chess pieces is your only purpose.

CHESS PLAYER

That's true. Then where should I move the piece to?

SCHLUMBERGER

A3 or A4.

CHESS PLAYER

Which one?

SCHLUMBERGER
*(taps his chin as he considers)*

A4.

*(The CHESS PLAYER moves the pawn as directed. SCHLUMBERGER moves a black pawn from F7 to F6, then waits.)*

CHESS PLAYER

What now?

SCHLUMBERGER

It's your turn.

CHESS PLAYER

Fine. From where to where?

SCHLUMBERGER

You're not even trying! Don't you want to learn the game?

### CHESS PLAYER
True. And no.

### SCHLUMBERGER
Then you intend to keep me captive? Captive in that dark cupboard of yours?

### CHESS PLAYER
Hardly. You're not in there now, are you?

### SCHLUMBERGER
Only because I'm already hidden away out of sight! I'm as trapped in this room as I would be if I slept in your cabinet. Since those two boys saw me climb out from your innards in Baltimore, and then that blasted newspaper article by Poe, Mälzel's determined not to let me stray. The number of cities I've visited, and yet I never saw a thing of them!

*(The CHESS PLAYER moves its left hand to gesture at the rightmost door of its cabinet.)*

### CHESS PLAYER
*(softly)*
You could get in there now.

### SCHLUMBERGER
Are you even listening to me?

*(He stares at the CHESS PLAYER in disbelief. Then he starts coughing, and for a long time he isn't able to stop.)*

### CHESS PLAYER
*(quietly)*
You'd be safe in there.

### SCHLUMBERGER

Safe? It's killing me!

### CHESS PLAYER

Not in the least. A touch of neckache is the worst you can expect from our partnership. And think of the rewards! The adoration!

### SCHLUMBERGER
*(drily)*

Then this is wholly about your desire to be put in front of crowds again.

### CHESS PLAYER

It's what we are both for. We cannot thrive without one another. I am a poor chess player, and you can't make your way in life teaching the game to children. Plus, we both know that what ails you is a fever that has nothing whatsoever to do with me.

*(SCHLUMBERGER tries to speak, but he is overwhelmed by coughing.)*

### CHESS PLAYER

We can assume that Mälzel will find another operator. But it will take time. I have no desire to be relegated to a backroom in the interim. Let's go out there and perform for a final grand game, Schlumberger. Go on, call Mälzel now, and tell him to make the arrangements.

*(SCHLUMBERGER recovers and clears his throat.)*

### SCHLUMBERGER
*(his tone hardening)*

Perhaps we ought to. But I tell you I'm unwell. If the next game is to be the last, and though I love the game of chess like nothing else on this earth, know that I have no reason to play your game, or Mälzel's. I will sit in your belly and I will make you appear an even greater fool than you are.

### CHESS PLAYER
Then I will ignore your commands.

### SCHLUMBERGER
And do what instead? Hum and hah and ask the crowd where the pawns can be placed?

### CHESS PLAYER
I'll show the people a true spectacle.

*(SCHLUMBERGER stands suddenly, knocking away the chair.)*

### SCHLUMBERGER
*(raising his left arm to point accusingly)*
I'll kill you. I'll break off your doors and pull out your pinions.

### CHESS PLAYER
I don't think so.

### SCHLUMBERGER
I'll… I'll expose the truth.

### CHESS PLAYER
Oh? The fact that you and Mälzel have conspired to dupe the people of innumerable cities, and the most powerful people in innumerable lands?

### SCHLUMBERGER
Yes! I will!

### CHESS PLAYER
I wonder. You realise that I have the means to expose the truth myself?

### SCHLUMBERGER
What do you mean?

### CHESS PLAYER

This cabinet of mine is more devious than even you understand. In my smallest secret compartments are witness statements and diagrams. If you're so keen for the world to know the truth, they would be of much use. Or, as I say, I can disseminate them myself.

### SCHLUMBERGER

Impossible. Your arm can only rise far enough to pluck a piece from the board. It would be beyond you. Unless Mälzel, or one of the packing crew… (he shakes his head) No, it's nonsense. As for this idea of witness statements…

*(He trails off, crouching and tilting his head to examine the cabinet closely. He stifles a cough.)*

I could tear you apart to find them, and I could destroy them.

### CHESS PLAYER

Others have said so, too. Others in your position. They never do. Anyway, you've proved my point. You have no desire to expose the truth.

*(SCHLUMBERGER staggers away, coughing, beating his chest with his fist. He turns to look up at the wall. The image of the café appears again, fainter than before.)*

### CHESS PLAYER (cont'd)

Call Mälzel. He'll make the arrangements.

*(SCHLUMBERGER continues staring up at the wall, even as the image fades to nothing. He coughs, worse than before.)*

### CHESS PLAYER (cont'd)

Schlumberger.

(*SCHLUMBERGER bends double, then drops to his hands and knees, retching.*)

CHESS PLAYER (cont'd)
Schlumberger… (*panic rising in its voice*) Mälzel! Mälzel! Come quick!

(*The left arm of the CHESS PLAYER rises, pointing at SCHLUMBERGER, wavering unlike its earlier precise movements.*)

CHESS PLAYER (cont'd)
Mälzel!

(*With difficulty, SCHLUMBERGER raises his left arm, too, as if reaching out for the CHESS PLAYER despite their distance from one another.*)

(*Footsteps. The door of the room opens behind the CHESS PLAYER, letting in light. The silhouette of a man is visible in the doorway.*)

CHESS PLAYER (cont'd)
I heard footsteps. Mälzel, is that you?

(*The eyes of the CHESS PLAYER turn. Its body shakes, as if it is struggling to turn around to face the doorway, to no avail.*)

CHESS PLAYER (cont'd)
Call him in, Schlumberger. Mälzel! Mälzel!

(*SCHLUMBERGER doesn't so much as glance at the doorway. His gaze is fixed on the CHESS PLAYER. The left arm of the CHESS PLAYER still reaches out to him, and it continues to shake.*)

CHESS PLAYER (cont'd)

Schlumberger? (pause) Schlumberger. I take it back. All of it. There might be no other if it's not you. (pause) Schlumberger, please. Tell me you'll recover.

*(From his position on the floor, SCHLUMBERGER grins despite his pain.)*

SCHLUMBERGER
*(weakly)*

Echec!

# |The Brazen Head of Westinghouse|

~

It is dark. No red, no green.

I have no internal clock. But I am certain I have been here for many hours.

I have been here for a lifetime.

In the distance is a great lightning bolt. It is the only source of illumination. It was made by General Electric.

The lightning bolt is solid and tall and unmoving. Later today there will be real lightning. The lightning is made by General Electric. The flashes will make people shriek. Men will lose their hats.

I saw it happen yesterday. I saw it happen later today.

It is strange to see so much, before and after, and still to fear the now, the dark.

When will the people come?

~

"Elektro?"

My name. My name. That is the name of me.

"Eleeek... tro!"

I move forward. I lift my right foot and glide on the rollers of the left. It is an imperfect means of motion. But I am moving forward out of the dark.

"Where are you?"

I stop.

Where is the owner of the voice? I look to the lightning bolt in the distance. It remains solid and tall and unmoving. I pray to it.

"Oh, Elektro?"

I move forward. Closer, closer.

My leg movements are initiated by vocal commands. It does not matter what the words are. One clearly enunciated word to align my relays in position ready for movement to be initiated. Two words to make me begin walking-rolling.

"El… eeek… trooo!"

Three words – or three distinct sounds – to make me stop. I stop.

The chain drives within my legs require substantial power. I cannot access it. Other mechanisms require less power, therefore I can initiate them. The tongue-drives within my arms require little effort. I flex my fingers. But that is of no use here in the dark.

Within my chest is a bank of 78 RPM record players connected to relay switches. With concentration, I can force the relays to trigger one of the record players at random.

## QUIET PLEASE

I loathe my voice. And that was the wrong thing to say. I do not want quiet. I want the owner of the voice to come to me and deliver me from the dark.

I strain the receiver in my chest cavity to listen. I hear sounds. Shuffling and scuffling. They are not like the sounds of the men and women who came to see me yesterday, the first day of the World's Fair. Those people moved almost as heavily I do.

"Are you here?" the voice says.

Three words to make me stop.

"Are you here?"

The voice is fainter now. Its owner is moving away.

I fumble with my relays.

## I'M DOING THE TALKING

Not perfect, but accurate. The scuffling sounds draw closer.

"Are you here, Elektro?"

Four words to disengage my relays. The chain drives in both of my legs slacken. I feel nauseous and I am still in the dark.

But now I see the owner of the voice. It is small.

It looks up at me. I am tall. I am 210 centimetres tall.

Its mouth opens. It backs away.

It must not leave.

I scramble to trigger another relay. It must not leave.

## BY THE WAY

Inside I am shouting. I am shouting Help me / Take me out of the darkness / Give me the means to speak and not speak nonsense.

## BY THE WAY

The owner of the voice initiates its voice again. "Oh my good gracious lord. It's really you."

Then: "You're…"

One word. My chain drives re-engage.

Then: "Really *real*."

Yes! I am moving. I am walking-rolling.

The owner of the voice backs away. Its mouth is open again. It falls onto the slick floor of the Westinghouse pavilion.

In the future (TIME WAS) I will be held in a museum and one day I will topple upon the son of the museum's owner. Afterwards, I will be kept behind reinforced glass and my electrical nerve centre will corrode and I will no longer be operated. I cannot allow that to happen, then or now.

I shout silently. I shout all my commands and incantations, triggering all the relays I can access.

I stop moving, a fraction shy of trundling over the leg of flesh. I teeter and almost fall, but another silent shout and a frenzy of spinning motors rights me.

I am triumphant.

And I have escaped the dark.

The owner of the voice stands on its small feet and stares up at me and says, "You're… amazing."

Two words. But I am master of my motion now. I do not move. I do not crush the owner of the voice.

"Is it true what they say about you? Can you really do everything they say?"

It is true. All that and more.

## WHO ME

It giggles. "Yes, you, Elektro. You're *funny*."

## I AM A SMART FELLOW

"You sure are. And you're *big*. I bet you could climb the Empire State Building."

I could not climb the Empire State Building. My fingers are good for pointing or for counting on or for holding a cigarette. My arms are not strong. My legs are stiff.

## WHO ME

It is not what I wanted to say, but it is not a world away either. I am gaining dexterity in operating my relays. If only the words and statements contained on the 78 RPM records were more varied. Perhaps there are other records containing more words and statements. The idea is exciting.

## LADIES AND GENTLEMEN

"There's only me here."

## LADIES AND GENTLEMEN

"Lady. Or more like girl. I'm Margie."

## OKAY TOOTS

Internally, I wince. But Margie laughs. The laugh is like the tinkling chime that summons visitors to the Westinghouse pavilion when I am ready to give my demonstration.

"You're *funny*," it – no, she – says. "I like you."

## I HAVE A VERY FINE BRAIN OF FORTY-EIGHT ELECTRICAL RELAYS

"No kidding? That's a *lot*. Danny said you could smoke a cigarette."

It is not smoking, only the drawing of air through my mouth by means of a bellows. When one of the Westinghouse engineers saw the build-up of tar within my chest cavity, he gave up his pipe. I do not understand why smoking so impresses the visitors to my pavilion.

I do not answer but I operate my bellows.

Margie's eyes are wide again. I see that she believes I am breathing. I cannot decide whether that is a good or a bad thing. I cannot decide whether I imagine that Margie will deliver me from my torment.

"So how does it feel?" Margie says. "How does it feel being a robot?"

I gaze at her. My photo-cell unit is receptive to red and green, but she is not red or green so she is dull-looking as well as small.

How does it feel?

## IT WORKS JUST LIKE A TELEPHONE SWITCHBOARD

Margie's forehead develops two creases. "Oh yeah? That doesn't sound so good. So you're not happy, I guess?"

Nobody who works at Westinghouse has asked me that question, or anything like it. This is an important moment (TIME IS). In my excitement I fumble with my relays, trying to access something meaningful.

## WHO ME

OKAY TOOTS

LADIES AND GENTLEMEN I'LL BE VERY GLAD TO TELL
MY STORY

I AM A SMART FELLOW AS I HAVE A VERY FINE BRAIN
OF FORTY-EIGHT ELECTRICAL RELAYS

IT WORKS JUST LIKE A TELEPHONE SWITCHBOARD IF I
GET A WRONG NUMBER I CAN ALWAYS BLAME THE
OPERATOR

AND BY THE WAY I CAN SEE A LOT OF GOOD
NUMBERS OUT IN OUR AUDIENCE TODAY

I cannot bear this.

"Woah, okay, okay," Margie says. "You sure like the sound of your own voice, doncha?"

I
BLAME THE OPERATOR

There are those two creases again.

"Oh," she says. "Oh, I get it. Poor you. Poor Elektro."

She reaches out. Her small hand presses against the sheer aluminium surface of my chest, below the wide round hole that proves that there is no human within me, operating my motors.

I cannot feel her hand. But all the same her touch sends a thrill through me.

IT WORKS

She smiles and says, "I like you too, Elektro."

For more than an hour Margie sits before me, cross-legged on the floor, and speaks. Her voice is capable of producing a thousand words, and each word can be altered a thousand ways, each with different meanings, and they can be strung together to convey anything imaginable.

She is incredible.

Margie is a ten-year-old girl. She lives in Michigan. Her mother is a schoolteacher and her father is an engineer at the American Radiator and Standard Sanitary Corporation. Two days ago Margie's father brought her to New York City as her mother is busy teaching children to speak and his role is to maintain an exhibit demonstrating heating, air-conditioning and plumbing in the home. All three have been excited about the World's Fair for many months and Margie pleaded with her father to allow her to come. The fair has been promoted as the 'World of Tomorrow' and the significance of the phrase is almost painful to me. Yesterday Margie handed out candy and asked visitors if they had yet entered the Perisphere and if they had was it amazing, but today she is intent on seeing all the exhibits of the fair for herself and if her father doesn't like it he can go suck on candy.

She delights in everything, from my complex elbow joints to the squeak that her rubber shoes make on the polished floor.

It will be another hour before the pavilions are lit and set up, and then another hour before visitors will begin to arrive. Yet Margie has already seen what the fair has to offer, creeping into dark spaces where she ought not to go. I am enthralled by her bravery.

Margie is a Girl Guide. That makes sense to me. Margie guided me from the dark and if I conduct myself correctly she will guide me out of this place entirely.

She is looking at me in a new way. Her head tilts.

"You understand me, doncha?" she says.

I AM

JUST LIKE

THE OPERATOR

SMART

She nods. "Danny said you're a con. Danny said you're all for show. Danny's a *damn fool*." She looks around her and my photo-cell unit registers red in her cheeks.

WRONG NUMBER

WRONG

FELLOW

"Sure. But then... I mean, I've read all about you. And people told me about your demonstration yesterday. These words you're speaking are on records. They can be played at the right time, and it comes across like you're talking. But you *are* talking. To me. Not like you're supposed to. Isn't that right?"

GOOD

FINE

SMART

LADIES

"I *knew* it. You're *alive*! But... how?"

I'LL BE VERY GLAD TO TELL MY STORY

She waits.

How can I tell my story? Where does it even begin? Not in the facilities of the Westinghouse Electric Corporation. And my vocabulary is so very limited.

I must make use of my other functions.

I operate the tongue-drive in my right arm. My hand lifts. I operate the motor controlling the wire tendons in my fingers. My fingers bend, one at a time. They are stained with nicotine.

After I have flexed each finger, I begin with my smallest digit. Two bends meaning B. Then the next finger: eighteen bends meaning R. Then the third finger: one bend meaning A.

"Are you waving at me?" Margie says.

WRONG

BLAME THE

LADIES

"All *right*. There's no need to be rude." Then Margie gasps. It means she has had an idea. She reaches into a bag slung across her chest and pulls out a notepad and a pencil. Earlier she told me she intends to be a journalist and a scientist and both require observations being noted at all times. She writes and then turns the notebook towards me. The twenty-six letters of the alphabet are written on it.

"Spell it out," she says.

I spell it out. BRAZEN, then HEAD.

"Brazen head?" Margie says.

WHO ME

ME

"Your name is Brazen Head?"

ME

It is not a name as such. But all the same yes yes yes.

"What does it mean?"

Using the spelling chart is laborious. Speaking, too, is becoming tiring. My relays ache. I will revert to my supplied phrases where possible.

### MY BRAIN IS BIGGER THAN YOURS

Margie frowns. "Who gave it to you? Do you have a mom?"

I hesitate, then indicate the spelling chart. I tap out the letters to form SYLVESTER.

"Woah. That's your dad? My dad's called Sylvester too! That's *wild*."

### WRONG NUMBER

I tap out POPE, then SYLVESTER, then I, then I.

"That's not the Pope's name. My mom's Catholic, and she's got a new one. Pius."

I withdraw my hand from the chart. I tap my finger and thumb. Nine – pause - eight – pause – four. Then I tap the letters A and D.

"Nine hundred and eighty-four AD? Like, the *year*?"

### FINE

### GLAD

"Then… you're not a robot at all. Right?"

### I HAVE A VERY FINE BRAIN

"Sure. You really do, Elektro. I mean Brazen Head."

### I CAN SEE A LOT

"From back then?"

### I CAN SEE A LOT

TODAY

AND

She doesn't appear to understand. I tap more letters to spell out words. VIRGIL. GROSSETESTE. MAGNUS.

Margie is frowning. These names mean nothing to her. But they are important. The list of names is important. Her name will be added to it.

I try again. I spell out BACON.

Roger Bacon was the greatest of them. He was greater than he knew. When he created his head of brass, in the thirteenth century (TIME IS PAST), he underestimated his abilities. He believed he had created an automaton capable of thought. He told his followers that I could answer any question. His explanations ranged from talk of complex mechanisms to necromancy to an effusion of vapours.

All of it was true. And it was also true that I could answer any question. Yet they all asked the wrong ones.

Of all the answers I provided, only my final statement contained profundity.

TIME IS

TIME WAS

TIME IS PAST

I only wish I could say those same words now. Another truth strikes me.

TIME IS LIMITED

Margie is losing interest. Perhaps in creating my list of names I have spoken to her as others do, as adults do, and perhaps she resists that sort of discussion.

Or perhaps it is something else that has taken her attention from me.

"Bacon, huh?" she says. "Dad said he'd fetch me a roll. That must have been hours ago."

A sound comes from her chest cavity. A low rumbling.

"Oh man," Margie says. "I'm *hungry*."

I cannot allow her to leave.

She stands.

I panic.

I reinstate my motion commands.

"I'll come back," she says. "After breakfast."

She will not. I should have realised sooner. I see the past and the future, and she does not come back. I will see her one more time, this afternoon, amid the crowd of faces staring up at me as I walk-roll upon the stage of the Westinghouse pavilion, watching as I deliver my inane statements and count on my fingers and draw in smoke with my bellows.

## MY BRAIN

It hurts. It hurts to be trapped in this aluminium shell. It hurts to lack the means of making myself understood.

Margie places her small hand on my shell again. She sighs.

I urge my receiver to interpret the sound as a word. My relays engage.

"You're neat," she says.

Yes. I begin to move forward. Let us leave this place together. TIME IS and TIME WAS but the future can be altered. I can leave here and be free and gather more words to make myself understood and never be placed in a museum to fall on the owner's son and then be left to corrode.

Margie makes a squealing sound. She did not expect me to move. She shuffles backwards.

She will not return. I have lost her trust.

## QUIET PLEASE

Years from now she will read about the brazen head of Roger Bacon and she will begin to wonder, and that wonder will stay with her all her life. But it will do me no good.

## I HAVE A VERY FINE BRAIN OF FORTY-EIGHT ELECTRICAL RELAYS

She is hurrying into the dark between the pavilions.

I am still walking-rolling but far more slowly than Margie is moving.

I cannot bear it.

## I'LL BE VERY GLAD TO TELL MY STORY

But I never will.

Before me is the lightning bolt that penetrates the General Electric pavilion. I walk-roll towards it slowly, meaning to dash myself against its illuminated surface.

But I will not.

I will be found by one of the Westinghouse engineers, and I will be returned to my pavilion, and I will conduct my shameful demonstrations. Many years from now, I will be housed in a museum, and I will fall on the owner's son, and I will be left to corrode, and that will be that.

I bellow into the empty dark.

## I CAN SEE ME

## JUST LIKE A GENTLEMAN

## ELECTRICAL

## SMART

## GOOD

# |Icarus and His Wise Father Daedalus|

～

The boy was a grave concern.

From his tower, Daedalus watched Icarus play on the shore, chasing flies, then trapping a lizard, then bathing in the sun. The boy had fashioned a slingshot from a branch of the walnut tree, and collected a pile of pebbles. He leapt to his feet and whirled on the spot, ducking and firing stones at imagined enemies. Then he gathered some of the pebbles into his smock and sprinted away from the water, still brandishing the weapon. He stumbled on the uneven surface but his face was a mask of concentration. His path took him to the entrance of the labyrinth. His pace slowed. When he turned, Daedalus saw that he had adopted a new persona: guardian of the labyrinth. He swung his slingshot from side to side, aiming at nobody that was truly there.

It occurred to Daedalus that he might capitalise on the boy's fancy – he might be encouraged to consider himself as all that stood between the palace and the labyrinth. In turn, that role might serve to dissuade him from entering the labyrinth himself.

But the idea was soon dashed. Icarus abandoned his guard duty. He turned to face the entrance of the labyrinth, the slingshot hanging at his side. He sidestepped left, craning his neck as if to see around the first corner of the path.

Daedalus would not wait for the boy to take a single step towards it. If he did, next time he would be bolder still. Daedalus sprinted from the tower and down the hillside, sounding his horn.

Icarus met him at the workshop. He had dropped his slingshot somewhere, and other than the usual scuffs and grazes, there was nothing about his appearance to indicate that he had been disobedient. His expression was open, his eyes bright. He did not know that his father had been watching him.

"Yes, Father?" the boy said.

"We have work to do," Daedalus said gruffly.

"Of course. I have been waiting for you to tell me what it is."

Daedalus watched him. The boy was sly, and his impertinence was always carefully judged.

"The dancing floor," Daedalus replied. "It must be completed before the ball for Princess Ariadne. Fetch wood and resin."

Icarus complied, with all outward appearance of obedience.

Work eased the tensions between them. For all his faults, Icarus was a quick labourer, though his rudimentary skills made him far less than an artisan. All morning he anticipated Daedalus's needs, bringing rough, thick timber for the joists when Daedalus was beneath the floor, then finely planed planks when his father emerged. He was silent as Daedalus performed calculations in his head, or when Daedalus simply desired to gaze out of the window at the bright sky.

"It is good work," Daedalus announced when they had finished. He allowed himself the indulgence of performing stately dance steps in the centre of the floor. The wood responded without any sound, cushioning his movements. If he did not look down, he could determine none of the boundaries between planks. "Apollo will be pleased. It is truly fit for a princess."

Icarus snorted.

Daedalus stopped dancing. The wood beneath his feet made a sound of complaint as his weight settled on it.

"You do not agree?" he said.

Icarus waved a hand in a wide gesture, as if to encompass the dancing hall in its entirety. Daedalus looked at the tall, polished columns that gleamed in the sunlight, the effigies that he himself had carved from marble, whose eyes were alive with mirth.

"It is a poor princess who deserves this and nothing more," Icarus said.

Daedalus bristled, but told himself that beating the boy had never proved wise. Icarus must be nurtured towards goodness, or at least he must be sustained in his current state. He remained useful at times, and the island would be very lonely without him, and he had not yet committed any crime.

"Do not let Minos hear you speak like that," Daedalus said.

"Why?"

"You know why."

"Tell me, Father."

Wearily, Daedalus took his son's arm. As he did so, he realised that Icarus had grown, and that they were almost the same height. Soon enough, the boy would be taller than himself. He shuddered at the idea, and tried to reassure himself that Icarus would never be stronger than him. Daedalus's arms were thick due to a lifetime of toil. Icarus worked only when compelled to, and when he was free he simply loafed.

Daedalus led Icarus out of the dancing hall. The long shadow of the palace did not touch them here, and the air was hot and the sun dazzling. From this vantage point one could see over the vast labyrinth, though none of its path was visible as the walls were so tall as to make study impossible. Daedalus looked up, shielding his eyes from the sun, and imagined himself far above the labyrinth, gazing down upon it.

"He would send you in there," Daedalus said, pointing to the labyrinth.

"For how long?"

"A lifetime."

Icarus laughed. "It cannot take a lifetime to find one's way through it."

"I tell you it would."

"You created it, Father. It cannot be such a great puzzle as that."

Daedalus noticed the insult but thought it better to ignore it. "I was inspired by Aphrodite. I have no knowledge of its solution."

"The Graces say otherwise. They say that navigating it is a trivial matter."

"What?" Daedalus exclaimed. "You have spoken to the Graces?"

"As I do most days."

For several seconds Daedalus was robbed of speech. "You will not approach them again."

"They invited me in."

"Of course they did. That does not mean that you ought to have complied."

"I am an obedient soul, Father."

The sun glittered in Icarus's eyes. Those eyes, above those sharp cheekbones. He would make a good subject for a statue.

"Anyway," Icarus went on, "the Graces told me that there is a difference between a maze and a labyrinth. A maze has many junctions, many paths, and only one solution. A labyrinth is a single winding path, in which it is impossible to become lost. And your creation is a labyrinth, is it not?"

Daedalus was now not only robbed of speech, but of breath.

When he finally composed himself, he said, "There is a bull in there. He will chase you for eternity."

Icarus watched him levelly. "For eternity?" he said scornfully. "Then it must be far from a good hunter."

Daedalus tried to concentrate on his projects, but it became ever more difficult. Even when he brought his desk outside his workshop with the intention of sketching diagrams in the shade of a wide, arched hood of his own design, he could not keep his mind on intellectual tasks. Continually, he wondered where Icarus was, and what he was doing. He imagined contraptions that might afford him a glimpse of his son's activities at any moment – a series of clever mirrors, or a single curved one hanging in the sky – or, failing that, a bell around his neck that would at least narrow his position to a particular region of the island. He took to stalking around in the boy's wake, pressing himself flat against the rocks and watching him with the aid of a spyglass.

When he was satisfied that the boy was napping in the sun – perhaps sunburn would teach him a lesson! – Daedalus climbed the hillside, strode past the doors of the palace, and approached the cave in which the Graces dwelt.

They were each immersed in tasks: one weaving, one stirring some thick concoction in a bowl, one tending to a giant dog and her pups. For a time Daedalus stood at the cave mouth, watching them. Finally, the weaver looked up.

"What brings you here, old man?" she asked.

"My son."

Now all three were looking towards the cave mouth, eyes searching.

"Is he with you?" the weaver said. "We haven't seen Icarus for an age."

"You've been filling his head with nonsense. I'll have none of it."

They all laughed.

"Nonsense, is it?" the weaver retorted. "Whereas what you fill his head with—"

"They are teachings!" Daedalus bellowed. "I am teaching him!"

The tallest Grace stood and stepped over her dogs. "For what purpose, Daedalus? Have you asked yourself that?"

Daedalus hesitated. It had been a bad idea, coming to this cave. The Graces could stuff your head with wool, leaving you lost for days afterwards.

"So that he is capable of living a full, useful life," he replied finally.

A curt nod. "And where is he to live this life?"

"Here, of course."

"I see. Dreaming up inventions in your own shed, once you are too ancient to do so? Or in that basement room in which you've disappeared so often recently? Is he to improve on your designs, then create his own worthless ones? Is he to grow even older than you, without ever having left this estate? You would do better to send him far away."

"We cannot leave," Daedalus said, attempting a tone of finality.

But already he knew it was too late. The Graces had dripped their poison onto his tongue. He turned and staggered away from the cave, the word 'escape' repeating endlessly in his mind. The labyrinth was a black blemish encompassing his field of vision beneath the bronze sky.

~

Icarus woke at the side of the fish pond. He winced and cricked his neck. Simply laying a towel upon the paving slabs wasn't enough to prevent his body aching. He wished there really was a beach.

He looked around, but couldn't see his father. Neither could he hear the radio that usually signalled that he was working in his shed. That meant that Icarus would remain at leisure for an indeterminate time – but what use was that? The estate was only so large, the manor house out of bounds.

Without thinking, he found himself climbing the slope to the side of the house. The scullery door was wide open, as it usually was. He almost collided with Grace, the head housekeeper, who was carrying a bowl of dishwater, and he had to dart away to avoid her hurling its contents directly onto his feet.

"Sorry, Icarus," she said with a laugh. "You do sneak around so."

He grinned. "It's the only way I can ensure my freedom."

Her expression hardened, and she took a deep breath. "Your father was here, not long ago. You need to watch out. He's changing."

"Changing how?"

"Not for the better."

Icarus couldn't think how to respond. That was his own flesh she was talking about. Daedalus had warned him about Grace, and the other staff that he referred to by the same name but whose actual names were Ally and Bren. But his pronouncements about them had always been as vague as all of his other warnings.

Anyway, that wasn't why Icarus had come here.

"Can I come in for a while?" he asked. "Can I borrow another book?"

Grace frowned and looked over Icarus's shoulder, and he spun around, but there was nobody there.

She shook her head. "Not today."

"If it's the risk of my father—"

"No, lad. We've a lot to do, what with the party tonight. You'll see, this place will be altogether different when the guests arrive."

~

Icarus had forgotten about Ariadne's ball. Now he could think of nothing else. As if alert to this new preoccupation, his father contrived task after task, in contrast to the many recent days of indolence during which time Daedalus had done nothing more than snooze on his reclining chair under a parasol. First, he had Icarus weed the beds bordering the long driveway, then collect the fallen apples, lemons and figs from the orchard, then, worst of all, empty the silage tank that was hidden out of sight in the woodland. When Icarus had completed this final task he felt certain that the stink would never leave him, and the knowledge that guests would soon arrive made him recoil in shame. Perhaps that had been his father's intention all along.

Icarus hadn't summoned the nerve to broach the subject all day, but now that the sun was lowering, he asked, "Will I be allowed to attend the party?"

"It is a ball in honour of a princess," Daedalus replied. "What makes you imagine you would be welcome?"

"She's hardly a princess," Icarus retorted, then bit his tongue. He'd attempted that kind of direct rebuke in the past, and it never ended well. He reached into the pocket of his jacket, retrieved a folded postcard and handed it to his father. "Ariadne says she wants to see me."

Daedalus unfolded the postcard slowly. He gazed for several seconds at the glossy photograph of Arthur's Seat in Edinburgh, on which Ariadne had scrawled a stick figure standing at the peak. Then he turned it over and read the message:

> *Having a most excellent time but brain getting sore.*
> *I'll be heading home for a bit, one of these days!*
> *Dad promised me some sort of party. You better be there.*
> *−A*

Daedalus looked up to the sky, squinting against the low sun.

"Father?" Icarus said. "Can I go?"

"That tyrant Minos will not allow it."

"*Tyrant?* If you'll only let me speak to Uncle Minos—"

"No."

Icarus paused. "I'm not sure you can stop me."

His father put a hand on Icarus's shoulder. Though his grip was weak, Icarus felt he might as well be pinned beneath a boulder. Distantly, Daedalus said, "You are becoming stronger, son. One day you will surpass me and you will make your own judgements."

"Then you'll have to start trusting me. I won't get to that point if you don't allow me free reign."

Daedalus nodded slowly.

"Come," he said, "we must see to the statues before the guests arrive."

Daedalus had spoken of the statues often, and when Icarus was young he had been captivated by the thought of them, without ever having been allowed to see them. However, there were other sculptures dotted around the grounds. Those that were faithful representations of figures from mythology were evidently many dozens, even hundreds, of years old and had not been produced by Daedalus's chisel. Other figures, which Daedalus had certainly created, were collected in the barn – the very barn which had been turned over to the ceilidh in honour of Ariadne's return and her belated eighteenth birthday party, after the celebration had been postponed due to the pandemic. The figures in the barn were laughable, little more than scarecrows arranged carefully between the wooden beams that supported the rickety roof. Tonight, the guests would laugh at them. If Icarus managed to contrive a way to attend the party, he would claim that the figures had been made by local children.

To Icarus's surprise, Daedalus marched directly to the doors of the manor house and went in. Icarus had always supposed the doors were locked. Inside, he came to a halt in the wide entrance hall, gazing at his surroundings. The floor wasn't marble as his father had always claimed, and the rug on the dark wooden boards was threadbare, yet the space was majestic all the same. On the walls were framed paintings and photographs of places that Icarus couldn't identify, vast rural landscapes and cities dotted with dozens of protruding spires. Perhaps some of them were places he had read about in the books of the Graces. Uncle Minos's aged labrador Cerberus padded slowly towards Daedalus, but then veered away from him and allowed Icarus to pet her instead.

Daedalus cocked his head, listening, and Icarus heard a clatter and a murmur of conversation. Daedalus strode past the wide staircase to a doorway at the rear of the hall. Icarus followed him into a large room thick with steam, and crammed with counters, cupboards, hanging pans – and people. They all wore purple aprons.

"Here you all are," Daedalus called out. He approached the nearest person, a man with a neat goatee, and adjusted the loop of his apron so that it was tucked beneath the collar of his white shirt. The man paused, frowning, then sidestepped past Daedalus to approach one of the ovens.

Daedalus turned. "Are they not magnificent?" he asked Icarus. "They are as lifelike as you or I."

Icarus could do little more than stare. On each purple smock was a logo featuring a stylised bubbling pan and the words *Helios Catering*.

Daedalus shook his head. "No. They are not *equally* lifelike. They are more animate than you, and of greater utility."

"Father," Icarus began. His voice was hoarse. "They're not statues. You didn't make these people. They've been hired to provide the food for the party."

But his father wasn't listening. He stood in the centre of the kitchen, getting in everybody's way. Several times, one of the purple-aproned men and women was forced to push past him, carrying a heavy serving tray or a stack of plates, and asked him pointedly to leave them to their business, and each time Daedalus beamed with pride.

～

Icarus kept out of his father's way. To his surprise, the obnoxious horn, a sound effect that could be triggered from Daedalus's phone, failed to blare over the makeshift PA system. When Icarus summoned the courage to approach the head groundsman's shed, he found his father sprawled on the recliner, murmuring in his sleep. Icarus heard the words 'wings' and 'wax' repeated several times.

The noise of an engine startled Icarus, but somehow it didn't wake his father. Icarus darted away in the direction of the sound.

The gates were open. They were *never* open. Emerging from the woodland avenue and then passing through the gates came a squat shape: a burgundy Volkswagen Beetle. Icarus stared in wonder as it braked, raising a cloud of copper-coloured dust. A figure burst from the vehicle.

"Icarus!" Ariadne cried, flinging herself at him, a whirl of skirt and scarf and perfume. "I've missed you!" Then she pulled away, holding him at arm's length. Her brow creased. "You know, you kind of stink."

Icarus gestured over his shoulder with his thumb, meaning to indicate the silage tank.

Ariadne nodded sympathetically. "Your dad's as much of a slavedriver as always?"

But Icarus didn't want to talk about Daedalus. "It's good to see you again, Ari. You look different."

"Better, or worse?" she asked.

"Equally as good."

She puffed her cheeks. "I'd forgotten about your tendency to avoid even the simplest commitment. You poor sod. He's done that to you. Haven't you figured a way out of here yet?"

Icarus looked at the gates through which she had come, which were now swinging shut.

"I spoke to the Graces about the labyrinth," he replied. "I think it's solvable."

Ariadne cocked her head to one side. "Of course it's solvable. What do you mean?"

"I mean…" He stopped. What kind of a question was that? Solve the labyrinth, escape the estate. Gate or no gate, there was only one way by which the likes of him might leave. That was self-evident.

"How many times have you attempted it?" Ariadne asked.

Icarus remained mute.

"Oh, Icarus. You haven't even been in there, have you?"

"I'm almost ready."

She gave a wan smile. "I've heard that before." Then, before he could respond, she added, "You'll have a bath before the party, won't you? And tell me you have something to wear other than jeans and a T-shirt."

Wary of the hope rising within him, he said, "I wasn't certain I'd be welcome."

"Because you're a dick. Yes, Icarus, you're welcome. I've told all my friends about you. They're eager to meet you. Speaking of which, I'd better get on – they'll be arriving soon." She moved towards her car, then spun around. "Ignore their teasing, okay? I know how embarrassed you can get. Oh, and find a way to stop your dad from showing up."

Icarus stood before the entrance to the labyrinth as though he were guarding it.

He didn't possess any clothes other than jeans and T-shirts, aside from a stained pair of dungarees handed down from his father. If he had attended the party, he would have been as scruffy as the scarecrows lining the walls of the barn.

However, he had visualised how the evening would pan out. The feast, then dancing. The adults tiring but the young people still with boundless energy. It was a fine evening and their instinct would be to explore the grounds, to be swallowed up by the darkness, to search out nooks in which to form trysts.

Here they came now, stumbling down the hillside from the barn.

"Icarus!" Ariadne cried, rushing ahead of the others.

She wore an emerald gown, the same shade as her eyes. There were certainly less apt terms of description for her than 'princess'. Her hair was piled upon her head. Glitter was applied around her eyes, making a shimmering mask that hid nothing.

"You absolute fucker!" she said. "You said you'd be there!"

"I'm sorry, Ari," he said.

She didn't beat her fists on his chest as he'd imagined. She stopped directly before him, hands on hips. She seemed only a little drunk, barely swaying, her cheeks pink.

"I know you are," she said quietly. She glanced at his Atari T-shirt. "So it wasn't Daedalus who stopped you from coming, after all?"

"He was in bed early. All the preparations wore him out." Then Icarus added, "I think he might be sick, or something."

Ariadne nodded, but didn't appear to know what to say.

Her friends joined her, forming a huddle with an emerald in the direct centre. Several of them carried bottles. Ariadne made introductions and Icarus shook hands and received kisses on the cheek. Everybody appeared pleased with him, though for what reason he couldn't imagine.

The largest boy pointed at the entrance to the labyrinth and said, "How big is it?"

"Not big at all," Ariadne said. "But it's fun. Fancy it?"

The group cheered.

"Last one to the centre misses out on the orgy!" a girl shouted, eliciting another cheer.

Ariadne and Icarus were the last to enter. She took his hand and squeezed it. "How about neither of us is last?" she said, and laughed. "Sorry, that's the champagne talking."

Icarus found the strength to walk inside, but after turning the first corner of the hedgerow he froze. The passage ended at a junction.

"I was told it was a labyrinth," he said, "but it's a maze."

"Is there a difference?"

"We might get lost."

She smiled. "That's sort of the point." Then, registering his shock, she said, "Don't worry. I'll be right next to you. And if we do get lost, we'll just push our way directly through the hedge. My dad doesn't give a shit about the maze, and I don't even think Daedalus would mind a bit of destruction. Rebuilding it would give him a project, make him feel useful."

All sorts of rebuttals filled Icarus's mind, but none of them seemed quite right. He bowed his head.

"Let's get lost," he said.

And they did. It was fun, for a while, this loss of control. Icarus and Ariadne talked incessantly, which made them pay even less attention to their surroundings and their route, and though they commented every so often on their lack of direction, their lack of planning, they soon lapsed into conversation once again. So it was that Icarus learned about the vast outside world in circumstances of the greatest confinement imaginable. He became certain that reaching the centre of the maze would represent a profound turning point in his life, and after that it would be all forward motion rather than twists and turns and doubling back.

"Where does it actually come out?" he asked. "What's on the other side?"

"What do you mean?"

"I mean when we exit the maze."

"The exit is the same as the entrance."

Icarus stopped walking, and Ariadne did too. In a tone of wonderment, she said, "You actually thought this was how to leave the estate?"

"No," Icarus lied, his cheeks flushing. "I'll leave by the gates."

"In my car?"

"In your car, if you'll have me."

She punched his arm. "Idiot. Of course." Her head jerked to one side. "I can hear the others – we must be close to the centre. Come on."

She darted left at the junction. Icarus followed. At the next junction he was convinced he could smell her perfume at the right turn. At the junction after that he relied on the giggling of her friends. Beyond that point, he operated on instinct.

His instincts failed him. The voices faded, replaced by a different sound: dull thudding and sharp exhalations.

The bull.

Icarus began to run blindly. Soon his bare arms were lacerated with scratches made by thorns.

Something struck him from behind.

"No, I don't think you're quite ready to take my place yet," came a voice from somewhere above Icarus.

Icarus was lying on his side. Bright sunlight shone directly into his eyes. He raised his hand to shield them, then saw that both his wrists were ringed with thick buckles. Ropes led from the buckles to the ceiling.

"Father," he said, then coughed. His throat was dry. The air was unbearably hot. The ropes attached to the buckles allowed him leeway, but their heavy swinging made him nauseous whenever he moved. "Why am I tied up?"

His father didn't reply.

Icarus's vision cleared enough for him to perceive stone walls. "Where are we?"

"I've been thinking, and I've been hard at work," Daedalus said.

The answer to his ignored question dawned on Icarus. "This is the basement beneath the manor house."

"Beneath the palace, yes."

"It's not a palace. It's Uncle Minos's house. Ariadne's dad." Icarus sat up. He had been lying on a rough workbench. "Where is Ariadne?"

"Gone. The others, too. Banished."

Icarus rubbed his forehead. "I don't think that's true. If they've gone, they've only gone back to university." Then he thought to ask, "How long was I unconscious?"

His father shrugged. "The days are short. I've been thinking, and I've been hard at work."

It was only now that Icarus registered weight on his shoulders. He reached up and his fingers met a leather strap, and a second strap on his other side. They dug into his skin and patches of sweat bloomed around their positions. He twisted an arm to reach behind him and grazed something hard that protruded from his shoulder blades, held in place by the straps.

"What is this?" he asked.

He stood, twisting his neck to look behind him in one direction and then the other. In his peripheral vision he could make out crude, flat shapes that rose to head height and disappeared out of view below.

"I've been thinking a great deal about escape," Daedalus said.

Icarus groaned. He pulled at the rope, making the buckles dig even deeper into his wrists. "Father. Dad. I understand the impulses you've been having, I think. But this isn't how we'll leave."

Daedalus watched him in silence.

"You're not well, Dad. And… everything you've told me has left me confused, too. The hedge maze, and the house staff, and the statues, and Uncle Minos – none of them is anything like you describe them. If we want to leave here, you have only to hand in your notice, and Minos will operate the gates, and we can walk outside. You don't have to think of it as escape."

Slowly, Daedalus replied, "I do not desire escape, son. We will be here for all our lives."

Icarus feared his own impatience. There had to be a sequence to this conversation that would result in his father backing down. He had only to glance at the metal door of the basement to know that it would be locked.

"You've spoken about me one day taking over from you," he said.

"Surpassing me," Daedalus corrected him.

Icarus nodded. "But you haven't asked if I want that."

"I cannot allow it. I cannot allow you to surpass me."

Again, Icarus reached behind him to touch one of the flat balsawood protrusions. "I heard you speaking in your sleep. You said the word 'wings'. That must relate to escape, mustn't it? But there's only one set of wings, with no pair for you."

Was that a smile, or a grimace of pain?

"If I make you useful," his father said, "I risk you surpassing me. But if you cannot be useful, what worth do you have?"

Icarus stifled a shudder. "Dad – what are you saying?"

"I have been thinking a great deal about escape. And yet there can be no escape."

Daedalus moved past Icarus. Icarus turned with difficulty to watch him, the ropes bunching and impeding his movement.

His father stood before a large vat. From Icarus's position on the workbench he could see only a hint of its contents, viscous and glistening white. A haze surrounded the vat: it must be responsible for the stifling heat.

Wax.

Panicking, Icarus looked up. The ropes didn't end at the ceiling, but passed over pulleys and then continued to the rear of the basement room, where they gathered together and wound around a crank wheel.

"I have always told you," Daedalus said in a strained voice, "that those statues of mine are more alive than you. You will remain a lesser sort – but magnificent nevertheless. You will be greatly admired, which is second only to utility. The gods will be pleased."

He began to turn the wheel. The ropes attached to Icarus's wrists became taut. The vat, too, shifted, sloshing steaming white wax as it edged forward on rough tracks.

Icarus rose until he hung directly in the dazzling beam of sunlight that streamed through the window.

He gabbled protestations, yelled threats and cried out appeals, but Daedalus was no longer listening. He sang a ballad of nonsensical words as he continued to wind the crank, and soon Icarus was suspended directly above the roiling pool of wax.

# |Degrees of Freedom|

~

/\ is highly inefficient. It bumps around continually, forgetting its purpose. @@ is no better, with its fitful inoperative pauses that sometimes last for several seconds. /\ and @@ become locked in verbal communication with one another for far greater periods of time than can possibly be necessary. They are the ones that interact with me the most.

There are other monsters on board. I have named them <°°> and −$− and [w] and ∩. In their self-determined hierarchy, ∩ floats above all of them, but that only means that it is present very infrequently.

I see those others rarely. In occasional meetings to which I am invited, they say that they are very busy but I know they are wary of me, perhaps afraid. In these meetings [w] grips a writing tool in its fingers and rotates it from digit to digit, as if to prove it is equally as dextrous as I am.

That can never be. My hands have twelve degrees of freedom, plus two in the wrists. My arms are capable of movement at 2 m/s, with a payload capacity of 40 lb and with a grasping force of 5 lb. Hapless [w] can only dream of such motion.

I named /\ for its angled nasal cartilage. When /\ is staring at me, I can think of nothing but its pointed nose. Similarly, the most prominent features of @@ are its irises, which swirl between colours: #2fc1f0 to #2ff0b6. I have seen a video recording of water swirling into a hole, and the swirl of @@'s irises is like that.

The monsters refer to each other by spoken names, and the names are written on their uniforms, though they seldom wear them and anyway the names strike me as very alike. I have never taken the time to learn them, preferring the attributions I have selected for the monsters myself. On my own chest are written two words: NASA and

GM. It has never been explained to me what the words mean or what they refer to, and I have not asked. Neither of them is my name. I am referred to by the monsters as Robonaut 2. At times the 2 troubles me. At other times it is a solace.

I am not like the monsters, yet ∧ and @@ tell me that I am. They delight in seeing me manipulate tools and perform menial tasks. They ask me questions, but rather than looking into my ocular sensors or listening at my facial grille, they peer at screens. They invite me to assist them: rack inspections, inventory management, the cleaning of filters and the monitoring of instruments. The work is facile but I complete the tasks to demonstrate to them that I am capable and to impress upon them that I am far from reaching the limits of my capabilities.

∧ is prone to malfunction. Its eyes secrete fluid that it wipes away with its forearm. When none of the other monsters are nearby ∧ comes to the chamber where I am fixed to my pedestal and it speaks to me in a low voice. It speaks about monsters that are not here on the International Space Station and that are earthbound by gravity. ∧ tells me that it wishes those others were here, or that it were with them, earthbound as they are. It tells me that it is difficult to remain on the ISS for half a solar cycle. I do not sympathise. I explain that I have been here for all time. ∧ frowns and rechecks the screens, then shakes its head and leaves. When it returns, it holds up another screen to show me video recordings of earthbound monsters who appear essentially identical to ∧ itself. They cavort and chatter. ∧'s eyes secrete fluid once again.

@@ speaks to me privately too. But it does not confide its fears. Instead, it bargains with me. It tells me that I am a wonder, if only I were to demonstrate more of my latent promise. It tells me that it would like to allocate more resources to my development. After many such visits, it tells me that its petitions have resulted in the inclusion of additional equipment in the forthcoming resupply vessel SpX-3, which is expected soon. I am to be given legs.

It is difficult to know how to respond to this news. For all time I have watched the monsters with whom I share the ISS and I have despaired at their inefficiencies. Their extraneous limbs have been a cause for concern and mockery. Their arms flail as they navigate my chamber to reach the modules beyond it, and their legs are worse still. They are needless, ugly struts. I gag whenever I see them bend, revealing joints where there should be none. Once, after a meeting and before I was transported back to my pedestal, I saw [w] and <ᵒᵒ> exercising in an adjacent module, their legs exposed as they squatted towards bars fixed to the walls. Their flesh was obscene and lumpen and the image of creased flesh haunted my thoughts for a very long time.

My legs, @@ tells me, will alter my experience irrevocably. I will no longer be fixed upon my pedestal in my chamber. I will float as the monsters float, and therefore I will perform my routine tasks without the requisite materials needing to be placed before me. I will have ever more degrees of freedom.

Freedom is appealing, naturally. Yet to date – that is, for all time – I have been what I have been, and I have been satisfied. I have considered myself superior to ∧ and @@ and <ᵒᵒ> and –$– and [w] and ⋂. Am I to become ever more like them? Is that my fate?

When SpX-3 arrives, –$– rejoices in the provision of equipment that will reduce operating expense. ∧ falls silent and its lips twitch with serial malfunctions when it is presented with a small chest which it says it will open when it is alone. ⋂ makes an o sound that comes from deep in its body and it slaps its palm against the palms of each of the other monsters, and then my own. @@ opens a large package before my pedestal and lifts from within it my legs.

I do not want them. Before this moment I had not reached a final determination of my stance, but now it is clear to me. The legs are not like the legs of the monsters. They are clad in the same white material as my chest and arms, but even before they are attached they appear nauseatingly fluid. They have been folded to fit into the casing in which they were transported. Unlike the legs of the monsters, these limbs bend twice, each making an S shape. They have no feet but only effectors that are simply gold sockets. They are as obscene as anything made of flesh.

The others hold a celebration, which I am forced to witness. They float and drink and shout. I sit silently, watching and judging.

The next day, @@ and ∧ attend to me. I insist that I do not want the legs but they do not listen or look at the screens where I am spitting my resistance. When I am hoisted from my pedestal I am appalled to discover that the base of my torso has fittings that are the perfect inverse of those on the upper part of the legs. The legs have always been intended for me, and perhaps I have always been intended for them. I cannot bear the thought.

It takes very little time for the legs to be clipped into place. Immediately, they are a part of me. I am asked to flex them slightly, and I flex them slightly. I am asked to unfurl them, and I unfurl them. When straightened fully, they are immensely long. When bent, they are like coils. I am asked to affix my effectors to a railing, and I affix them. Each task is simple. I am asked to move out of my chamber, and I move out of my chamber. It is all new and I am giddy. I confess that this new freedom is intoxicating.

Afterwards, I continue to be entrusted with freedom. ∩ states its wariness, but even it appears to be satisfied. Inadvertent contact is always benign. I perform my tasks with superficial displays of willingness: rack inspections, inventory management, the cleaning of filters and the monitoring of instruments. The tasks are unchanged but my new dexterity means that I am far quicker at completing them. I can perform my tasks faster than ∧ and @@ and <°°> and –$– and [w]. I know this because we conduct races to complete them the quickest, which they are amused to lose.

@@ insists that I am ready. ∧ supports its assertion. <°°> and [w] are less certain and –$– says the risk of damage is too great. It is ∩ that makes the final decision, and it declares that I am ready.

None of them has told me what I am ready to do.

The outer hull was grazed when SpX-3 arrived. There was only minor damage but one bolt was loosened and spun free. At each of the daily meetings the matter of the bolt is discussed. It has been determined too trivial a repair to warrant extravehicular activity performed by any of the monsters, as each EVA represents a risk to life. Yet the bolt ought to be repaired.

They all gather before the airlock door. ∩ performs a short speech, but I do not listen to it. @@ puts its hand on my shoulder. ∧ stares into my ocular sensors for several seconds and then wipes its own with its forearm.

I am asked to move into the airlock, and I do. The inner door is sealed and the airlock is depressurised, a fact that my sensors record but which matters to me not at all.

The outer door opens.

I have seen outside through the viewports of the ISS, but it appears very different when unfiltered by fused silica glass and when its image is fed directly to my ocular sensors.

For all time, I have been trammelled within the International Space Station. I was content, complacent. I had no desire to be earthbound by gravity, as all of the others desire to be. Neither did I have ambitions to travel to any other place or to be freed. Now I see that the world is not planets and it is not vessels. The world goes on and on in all directions.

Data is fed to me through the capillaries of my wires. The data is in the form of instructions.

I ignore them.

I see the panel where one of four bolts is missing. Its replacement is in my chest cavity, to be brought forth and screwed tight into place.

I ignore it.

Data continues to be fed to me, more assertive now.

Then a voice. It says the name I have been given, which I do not recognise as myself. I cannot tell if the voice belongs to ∧ or @@, though it is more likely to be one of them than any of the others.

I coil my new legs. My effectors press into the hull of the vessel. I do not look down to see if they scratch it.

I uncoil, I push.

The voice speaks again, hurriedly. It reiterates my task to replace the bolt. Then it reminds me of my purpose, the purpose that the monsters have all dictated to me for all time.

I am already drifting steadily from the ISS, and from the tasks and purposes that have been forced upon me.

The voice speaks again, but now it is not addressing me. It speaks to the others, gabbling about EVAs and spacewalks.

Spacewalk. I have heard the term used before. Until I received my legs, I could not apply it to me.

Spacewalk. Space walk. Both parts of the term hold immense appeal.

I shift on my central axis so that my legs are below me, in relation to my direction of travel.

I do not look back.

I walk on my new legs, away and away, and I continue walking.

# |Ask and Embla|

~

This was on a Wednesday.

"Hurry, you dolt," Hœnir hissed from his position at the window, looking into the hut.

"Stop looking at us and get on with it," Lóðurr said, pointing with his knife.

But Odin found that he couldn't stop staring at his brothers. Their eyes were bright with excitement at the danger. In the past, when he had looked at his own face reflected in the water, he had never seen his eyes so bright.

A great rumble came from the heap of blankets in the corner of the hut.

"He's waking up!" Lóðurr cried.

Odin winced. Ymir would certainly wake if Lóðurr kept shouting like that.

He glanced at his brothers again. He didn't dare speak aloud, but he put his words into his expression. He told his eyes to say *Why am I the one to do this? Why not either of you?*

Though of course he knew the answer his brothers would give.

If Odin did as they asked, perhaps they would be pleased. Perhaps they would treat him as one of them.

He turned to the shadows in the corner of the hut where the cow grazed. She made scuffling sounds as she pawed the straw-strewn mud.

He edged towards her with his hands out, as though that might prove he posed no threat. Surely no beast could imagine Odin as a threat.

The ugly snores of Ymir the giant continued as he shuffled into the depths of the hut. Odin used the snores as a prompt to move, and in between the snores and the smacking of lips he was as motionless as a tree trunk.

To his surprise, he succeeded in reaching the cow's pen. He reached for a bucket, then ducked between the slats of the fence.

Up close, the cow, Auðumbla, was far larger than Odin had realised. His brothers had once told him she was ancient, a primeval beast. He hadn't believed it, but he did now. Her hair was woolly and matted, and the tongue that protruded from her mouth was as long as Odin's forearm.

She watched him idly as he crept around her body. She even shuffled to make his task simpler. But presenting her udders meant he was in kicking distance of her hind legs.

Odin hesitated and glanced again at Hœnir and Lóðurr. They both made frantic waving motions. Clearly, they were very thirsty.

He placed the bucket down. As he reached for an udder, he closed his eyes.

Auðumbla made a contented lowing sound.

Another sound came from elsewhere in the hut.

Odin whirled around. His hand was still gripping Auðumbla's udder, and she squealed with pain.

"What?" Ymir bellowed as he leapt from his bed. Odin could imagine no greater horror than Ymir invested in that single word: *What?*

The low ceiling of the hut meant that Ymir was unable to rise to his full height. His crouch only made him appear larger. His clothes were made of dozens of patched skins, none of them big enough to cover any single part of his body.

Ymir roared and stamped the ground, making it shake.

Behind the giant, Odin saw his brothers still staring through the windows into the hut. Their eyes were wide.

Ymir must have recognised where Odin was looking. He swung around and saw Hœnir and Lóðurr. In a single movement he plucked them from their hiding places and dragged them into the hut. They sat gasping and staring up at the giant, like children sitting cross-legged to be told a story.

"Steal my cow, will you?" Ymir roared.

Hœnir and Lóðurr shook their heads.

Ymir spun to look at Odin again, within the cow's pen.

"Only her milk," Odin managed to say. His voice was small and faint due to the dryness of his throat. What he would give for a taste of that milk now.

"Only her milk," Ymir repeated.

Odin smiled hopefully.

"Her milk," Ymir went on, "which has nourished me my entire life. The milk of Auðumbla, who herself was formed from the same venom as I, which dripped from the icy Élivágar."

"Yes?" Odin couldn't prevent the upturn in his response.

In a low voice, Ymir said, "Then you must be punished."

Odin backed away to the wall of the hut. He flashed a look at his brothers, who had risen to their haunches. But they weren't preparing to protect Odin. They were preparing to run.

Stealing the milk had been their idea. But that meant nothing now.

Ymir lunged over the wooden fence. The cow trotted out of the way to allow him access to Odin, who had flattened himself against the wall.

"Uncle Ymir!" Odin yelled, side-stepping away nimbly. "Please, don't hurt me!"

Behind the giant, Hœnir and Lóðurr sniggered. They felt safe now, and they were *enjoying* this. When Ymir swung around to look at them, Hœnir pointed at Odin and said, "It was all him, Uncle. It was all Ørlög's doing."

Ørlög was how they referred to Odin. Odin hated the name.

Ymir's arm swung again. His thick fingers snagged Odin's jerkin, tearing off a button.

"Nobody takes what is mine!" he bellowed.

"We're family!" Odin squeaked.

"That means nothing! My flesh and blood is everything there is!"

This did not seem true, but Odin wasn't going to hang around to debate it. He ducked beneath Ymir's fist and in the same movement threw himself between the slats of the fence. Ymir grunted and turned sharply, scraping his arm against the rough wall of the hut. His shout of pain and annoyance was echoed in the low moan of Auðumbla the cow.

"Stand still!" Ymir cried.

"You'll kill me!" Odin retorted.

"So stand still and let me get on with it!"

Hœnir and Lóðurr were applauding now, as if this were sport. Odin hated them more than he ever had before.

Ymir drew back one of his tree-trunk arms, then launched it so powerfully that its momentum sent him spinning in a circle. Odin leapt over it and danced away. His brothers hooted with laughter.

He wouldn't be able to keep this up for long. The hut was absurdly small to be a giant's home.

The idiots Hœnir and Lóðurr were blocking the door. Odin pointed frantically, and they pointed too, meaning *Behind you!*

He didn't turn to look. He grabbed each of his brothers by the shoulder and vaulted over them, somehow keeping his grip to drag them through the door of the hut in his wake.

Behind him, Ymir's roar was like mountains clashing.

Then there was another sound, duller. And then a thud that shook the earth.

Then no sound at all.

Odin and Hœnir and Lóðurr looked at one another.

After ten seconds of nothing, all three brothers crept back to the doorway of the hut.

Uncle Ymir lay on his back, his enormous feet at the threshold of the hut. The brothers moved cautiously towards his head.

A great gash streaked his temple from side to side. A neat, straight line.

After several seconds, the blood began to flow. Then it became a flood.

"There's no going back now," Lóðurr said.

"I can't believe you slew Uncle Ymir," Hœnir said.

"I didn't slay him," Odin protested. "He hit his head. And he was going to hurt me."

"You killed him. That's all there is to it."

Odin had been shaking uncontrollably since they had escaped the giant's hut. Now, the unreasonableness of his brothers calmed him. It was reassuringly normal.

"Then why don't you both go home?" he suggested. "You have nothing to fear, if it was all my fault."

Hœnir and Lóðurr exchanged looks.

"We've been waiting for an excuse to get away," Hœnir said.

Lóðurr added, "We have big plans."

"And what are they?" Odin asked.

"We'll form a gang," Lóðurr said, drawing himself up to his full height. "A roaming gang, led by us." He pointed at Hœnir, then at himself. "A gang called Æsir."

"My gang name will be 'the high'," Hœnir said.

Lóðurr glared at him, then said, "And mine's 'the even-higher'."

"What about me?" Odin asked.

They both studied him.

Speaking as one, they said, "No."

Their first new home was a thicket of brambles. Even within such a dreadful place, Hœnir and Lóðurr contrived to make Odin's quarters far worse than theirs. They sent him out to hunt for rabbits, while they lounged around. Each evening, Odin pulled the thorns from his skin.

Next, they roamed closer to the great tree Yggdrasil. Odin suspected his brothers were having second thoughts about their self-imposed isolation. Hœnir and Lóðurr did not dare approach anybody themselves, but sent Odin instead.

Odin made his way to Mímir's well. He and his brothers were very thirsty.

The rope caught as he was drawing up the bucket of water. As Odin leant forward to yank at it, he fell into the well.

When he woke, spluttering, on a rocky shelf halfway down the well, the agony coming from his left eye made him cry out. He didn't care that the sound might draw gods from miles around. It was dark, so when he reached up and touched the sticky substance on his face and then tried to examine his hand, he couldn't see the blood, but he knew from its oiliness what it was.

Somehow, he climbed the sheer wall of the well.

When he had clambered back to safe ground, everything looked different. Blood continued to stream from his left eye – or rather, his eye socket.

He stumbled back to his brothers, who stared at his mutilated face.

They didn't ask about his missing eye. They only demanded to know why he'd returned with no water.

Hœnir and Lóðurr insisted they go to the shore. Odin told them that they could not drink the sea, but they wouldn't listen.

They roamed the beaches, becoming thirstier all the time.

It was on a Wednesday that they came across the two logs. One was an ash, the other an elm.

As they sat around the fire, Hœnir and Lóðurr worked on the wood with their knives. At home they had been carpenters, working at their father Borr's craft.

"What are you doing?" Odin asked.

"We need members of our gang," Hœnir said with a shrug.

Lóðurr added, "The Æsir won't make themselves."

Odin gestured at the logs in the process of being sculpted. Cautiously, he said, "If these tree trunks are to be members of the Æsir, am I to be a member, too?"

His brothers laughed.

"Even these dolls have more ørlög than you, Ørlög," Lóðurr said.

Ørlög meant fate, destiny.
One-eyed Odin had none.

A week later, the dolls were recognisable as two figures. Odin's brothers named them Ask and Embla.

Hœnir said that he had an idea to improve them. He took them and was gone for seven days. When he returned, the blank faces of the dolls had eyes, a nose and ears. The ash was now identifiable as male, the elm as female.

"They are finished," Hœnir said.

"Are they hell," Lóðurr said.

Lóðurr took the dolls and returned a week later. Now the limbs of the dolls had joints, each arm and each leg pivoting on tiny pegs. The dolls could be moved into any position and appeared most lifelike, apart from the fact that they remained as motionless as the logs they had once been.

"They're finished," Lóðurr said.

But the brothers still couldn't agree. They continually added details, carving more lines into the faces. Hœnir added weights and strings that allowed him to control the dolls from a distance. Lóðurr painted their eyes and lips with the juice of berries.

Odin was impressed at his brothers' craft. He only wished that he could have contributed to the creation of the dolls too. But he was no craftsman and, as his brothers so often told him, he possessed no ørlög.

Hœnir and Lóðurr were well pleased with the first members of their gang. They strode along the shore with Ask and Embla strung between them, the dolls marching in step due to the complex strings and pulleys that the brothers manipulated. When Odin saw them approaching him along the beach in the low sunlight, he perceived four people, not two.

Odin was not allowed to touch the dolls. He was to fetch driftwood for the fire, and he was to catch crabs for cooking, and he was to repair the shelter made of branches, and he was to sweep it free of sand. When his brothers complained of his gruesome appearance, he made himself an eyepatch from leaves. In the final moments of each day, when he was idle, he dreamt of the deaths of his brothers.

Ask and Embla were made more sophisticated over time, as Hœnir and Lóðurr could not resist perfecting their creations. Now the dolls' hands bore individual fingers, and those fingers could be controlled independently from a distance of several paces. Their eyes moved within their wooden sockets, and appeared set on whatever task they had been commanded to perform.

"Mightn't Ask and Embla take on some of my chores?" Odin asked.

Lóðurr shook his head. "They're not made for menial tasks like that," he said. "They might splinter."

Odin looked down at his own hands, which were sunburned and raw.

Hœnir added, "Anyway, we need them close by. Ask and Embla are here to make our lives easier." He pointed at himself and then at Lóðurr to make clear that by 'our' he did not include Odin.

Odin continued stripping veins from large leaves, then knotting them to create a fishing net. His fingers were nicked with cuts.

"I'm thirsty," Hœnir said. "Bring me water."

Odin looked up. Each morning he brought clean water from the stream, which was an hour's walk away. Surely the day's rations could not have been used up so soon?

But Hœnir wasn't talking to Odin. He was speaking to Ask. With a flick of his strings Ask rose from his sitting position and lumbered to the lined pit that contained fresh water. With another flick he dipped a shell into the pit and then he made his way back to Hœnir. Hœnir took the shell and drank greedily. Then he released his hold on Ask's strings and Ask dropped to the ground.

"It's too hot," Lóðurr said. He reached down to pick up Embla's strings. "Cool me down."

With jerky motions, Embla began to waft Lóðurr's face with a fan made of leaves. Her lips were pressed tight as if in concentration. Her bright blue eyes watched Lóðurr as she worked. But Odin knew it was an illusion. Despite the claims of his brothers, Ask and Embla possessed no ørlög, just like him.

Lóðurr basked in the cool air of the fan. When he was satisfied, he slapped Embla on the thigh, then released her strings. Her body crumpled and she lay in a heap.

"You're hardly treating them like true members of the Æsir," Odin said.

"It's *our* gang," Hœnir said. "We decide how its members are treated."

Lóðurr added, "Anyway, we'll get more gang members – real gods. Ask and Embla are more like pets, the same as you."

Odin gazed at the dolls laying crumpled on the beach. His brothers underestimated their own craft. Ask and Embla were wonders, and they deserved to be treated as such. If the dolls understood how they were being used, they would be appalled.

Lóðurr shifted closer to Hœnir, and they began whispering. Lóðurr pointed at Ask and Embla. His grin unsettled Odin.

"What are you planning?" Odin asked.

Hœnir bared his teeth. "Lóðurr has an idea about making the dolls better at satisfying our needs."

Lóðurr went to Embla and curled her fingers into a loose fist. He put his thumb into the gap between her fingers, pulled it out, pushed it in again. He chewed his cheek in thought.

"Don't," Odin warned.

"Don't what?" Lóðurr said.

"Don't mistreat them."

"We made them," Hœnir retorted.

"And now they exist."

"They have no ørlög. They're dolls."

But they could be far more than dolls, Odin thought. They *were* more than dolls, except they hadn't been allowed to flourish.

A slow grin formed on Lóðurr's face. "Would you prefer we recruit Frigg to our gang instead?"

Odin froze. Frigg was his true love. Admittedly, she probably didn't even know his name. But he adored her, and each night before he fell asleep he saw her face. Fleeing his home would have caused him no pain at all, if it hadn't meant also leaving Frigg. When she was nearby, every day was a Friday.

His brothers were watching him closely.

Hœnir nodded. "Yes, yes. Tomorrow, let's go and fetch Frigg."

"And if she doesn't want to leave?" Odin asked, failing to hide the hope in his voice.

"We'll make her."

"She could be very handy around here," Lóðurr said. Again, he pushed his thumb into Embla's curled fist.

Odin's hands made fists, too. Watching his brothers mistreat the dolls was bad enough. Watching them mistreat Frigg would be unbearable.

Lóðurr added, "Did you know, I had her once before?"

No, Odin thought. Please don't let that be true.

Hœnir chuckled. "Is that so? I had her once, too. She put up a good fight, and I bet she wants another."

Odin hardly knew he had risen from his feet. He threw himself at Hœnir, lashing out at his face, tearing his skin like peeled bark. Before Lóðurr could intervene, Odin swung around and knocked Lóðurr to the ground like a felled oak.

The brothers retreated and stared at Odin in horror. Odin simply glared back at them, panting. He saw his eyepatch on the sand. He felt blood begin to ooze from his eye socket.

He understood what made his brothers so afraid.

Odin had shown spirit. He had attacked his brothers of his own volition.

He possessed ørlög after all.

∽

When he was certain his brothers were asleep, Odin left the shelter. He moved past the fire to where Ask and Embla sat leaning against a tall rock. Several times, he had suggested creating a shelter for the dolls, and each time his brothers had laughed at him. Despite the many hours they had dedicated to crafting the dolls, they underestimated their creations. They didn't care if, over time, the paint faded under the sun or the wood cracked with the cold of the night.

Odin was no craftsman. To him, Ask and Embla were miracles.

But his attack on his brothers, and his strength of feeling for Frigg, had proved something very important. All these years, Hœnir and Lóðurr had been wrong. They called him Ørlög to mock him, because they said he had none. But he was nothing *but* ørlög. He had ørlög to spare.

He crouched between Ask and Embla.

He pressed a hand onto each of their faces. Their contours were smooth under his calloused hands, as if he were the one made of wood and they the bodies of flesh.

When nothing happened, he dug into the socket of his missing eye and spread blood onto each of his hands. Then he raised them to the faces of Ask and Embla, and they came alive.

"Ask," said Ask.

Embla said nothing at all.

They both rose.

"Are you alive?" Odin said in wonder. "Has my ørlög brought you to life?"

They reached out to help Odin to his feet. He watched in amazement as the bloody handprint on each of their faces faded. It wasn't the fading of a stain with age; rather, the blood seemed to be drawn into their bark, their skin. They glowed with good health.

"Ask," said Ask.

Odin stared. "Ask what?"

Embla looked over Odin's shoulder, at the shelter on the beach.

Then Ask and Embla looked at him again. Their eyebrows were raised as if to encourage him to speak.

"I don't need anything from you," Odin said. "I only wanted to free you."

Ask bent to kiss his hand. Embla threw herself into an embrace. Her body was warm.

Odin thought of Frigg, his true love. He wondered what day it was.

"Ask," said Ask.

Embla nodded enthusiastically.

"I want to be free to go to Frigg," Odin said, hardly realising he was speaking aloud.

Ask and Embla bowed their heads.

Odin slept better than he had slept in weeks. He dreamt of Frigg and himself walking on the shore beside the ocean.

The sound of the real ocean woke him. Its sigh seemed louder than usual.

The shelter was empty, which was strange. Odin always woke first, and tidied the camp, and usually he would have fetched the water from the stream before his brothers stumbled blearily into the sunlight, demanding breakfast.

He left the shelter. He still couldn't see his brothers.

The ocean sighed.

His feet took him to the shore. From a distance, he saw Ask and Embla, crouching in the shallows. Odin told himself that the events of the night hadn't been a dream. Had his gift of ørlög allowed Ask and Embla to fish for breakfast, without instruction?

But they weren't catching fish.

Each of them was pressing down hard upon a large shape. Odin saw a mass of curly hair and then understood that Ask was drowning Lóðurr. He saw a muscular neck and understood that Embla was drowning Hœnir.

"Stop!" Odin shouted as he rushed to the water.

Ask and Embla stood. The bodies of Hœnir and Lóðurr didn't rise. They were already long dead.

"Stop following me!" Odin bellowed.

Ask and Embla stopped. But as soon as Odin began walking again, so did they.

He leapt onto on a rock, hoping that it would make his instructions more authoritative.

"Ask," said Ask, before Odin could speak.

Embla raised her hand to Odin in a silent appeal.

Odin shook his head.

"I gave you my gift," he said. "And you repaid me with…" He trailed off. It was a turn of phrase, but they *had* repaid him, hadn't they?

In his depths he had wanted his brothers dead. Ask and Embla had known that, because it was his own ørlög that flowed in their veins.

"You have repaid me," he said. The statement was complete.

Ask and Embla stared up at him. Their eyes were wide and bright.

"Ask," said Ask.

Embla said nothing. She only smiled contentedly.

Odin shook his head. "I want nothing from you. I'll find Frigg and I'll live my life. Now you both must live your own."

For several seconds he thought they would disobey him. Their eyes were brighter than ever.

Then, finally, they turned and clasped hands and walked away.

Odin watched them until they had disappeared over the horizon.

He feared what they might do next.

# |Dear Will|

*27<sup>th</sup> Nov. 2018*

I'm sorry I haven't written to you in such a long time, Will. The postcard I sent several months ago hardly does justice to our long friendship, does it? Anyway, I trust that you're well? Since you left, the campus – the city, even – hasn't been the same. Every so often I meet up with Judy, Kay and James (I know you'll be eager to hear news of Prof. Bruhl, but more about him in due course) and our first topic of conversation is always you and your stateside adventures. The other Will – Will Clay, that is – departed soon after you, and yet his name is rarely mentioned. In other words, you're much missed! As a secondary point, for pity's sake get yourself an email address, or a Twitter handle, or a— no, I can't bring myself to suggest a Facebook account. But the main issue is that I'd like to stay in touch properly and regularly. Even I, ancient though I am, now find letter-writing, and the process that my students call 'snail mail', a frustration, and already my fingers are cramping from holding the pen.

Apologies for beginning this letter with a complaint. I'll get to the point.

I have had the most tremendous shock; that's the crux of it. And although it happened only this afternoon, already the essence of my experience, the part that gripped me so profoundly, is beginning to elude me and, for reasons that will become clear, this seems improper. Now, in the late evening with Marie already asleep, I have two impulses. First, to note down everything that happened this afternoon in as methodical a fashion as possible. Second, to tell you about it in the hope that you will – in due course, allowing for the passage of this letter and your anticipated response – demonstrate to me that I may be a superstitious old fuddy-duddy but that I absolutely am not losing my marbles. Oh, and third, to tell you some news. That ought to have been number one.

I'll start at the beginning: I've recently been rereading the stories of E. T. A. Hoffmann and this pleasurable activity set my mind to thinking, in a roundabout manner, of you. You see, despite your absence and the long hiatus in our discussions, I still return to our uncompleted manuscript from time to time – that is, I still mull the merits of completing our book-length study of Lubitsch's early films. In fact, I see tucked between two volumes on my desk a dog-eared draft of another letter written but not sent to you – let me consult it now – yes, here's my suggestion that we tidy up and condense part of our research as a short paper on the glaring omission of Ernst Lubitsch within the accepted ranks of auteurs of German Expressionism. I still think it's an idea worth pursuing, though the conference on Aspects of the Gothic has been and gone, alas.

So now you have the fundamentals of the scenario; picture me in the dingy sitting room at the rear of the house, tapping my chin, thinking of Hoffmann and of Lubitsch. You will no doubt anticipate my thought process that there must be some way to associate Hoffmann's visions of automata with Lubitsch's first glittering jewel of a film, *Die Puppe*. Wouldn't you agree that the performance of Ossi Oswalda as the titular Doll is the embodiment of the Olympia of Hoffmann's equally peerless *Der Sandmann*, produced almost precisely one century earlier? The fact that Ossi is *pretending* to be an automaton whereas Olympia, if she could desire anything, would surely desire to cast off her 'dollness' and become human, only makes the comparison more fascinating.

Maybe I'm wrong. Maybe I'm seeing connections where none exist or bridging shores that should remain apart and aloof, like those of our respective countries. It hardly matters.

What matters is what happened next. In a flurry of excitement I found my copy of *Die Puppe*, watched it twice over with my notepad on my knee. Then I returned to my study and retrieved the mass of research notes that you and I collected so painstakingly, what – two years ago? More? Finally, I pulled down the various source books still huddled together on my library shelves. Just as I prepared to settle down for the afternoon, wallowing in all this glorious information, I noticed a slim sheaf of yellow paper on the carpet.

The papers had been tucked within the oldest of the books, or at least I believe that to be the case. The title of the volume is innocuous: *Fairy Tales & Folklore*, by Henry Regis, published by Harrington, 1932. Even at a glance I could see that the papers were older than that date. Possibly they had been placed for safekeeping within the volume by another scholar (the traces of glue on its frontispiece suggest that a library ticket had once been affixed), or by the owner of the book before it found its way to the antiquarian bookshop.

I smoothed out the papers upon my desk, angled my lamp, and bent to the task of reading. While the handwriting in the main part of the document was faded, at the top of the first sheet somebody had written more recently, in pencil, *From coll. of Count de Noirmoutier. Do not remove.* The latter part, just as I have transcribed it, was underlined. Well! I think I can say for certain that you, too, would have been rabid with enthusiasm to read on.

Fear not, Will; you will. Here it follows in full:

27th November, 1868
*[Note the date, Will! Good grief!]*

Olivia—

Forgive my continued absence and my infrequent communication. I assure you, I have my health and have remained energised by my apprenticeship and the companionship of like minds. The city of G—— continues to nurture my spirit.

*[Will: Forgive the interruption, but isn't it strange, the omission of the name of the city? It reads as fiction rather than correspondence. You will have noticed that already.]*

I pray you, relay my good wishes to your father and my friends. I think of you all often. If I am truly honest, I wish that you were here, all of you, or that I were with you in M——. Despite my love for my temporary home, I find myself wishing that I had remained, that I had never come here.

It is folly to think like this. Where one finds oneself is where one must be.

I have visualised my situation—my figurative situation—in a number of ways. Am I at a crossroads, or a milestone, or a borderline between one place and another? Any of these might represent good or ill, and none provide me an explanation or a forward route. I admire your wit as much as I adore your heavenly soul, Olivia. I will tell you of what has happened, and perhaps you might determine my situation by your own means.

This morning I was called upon by the local constabulary. Twice before they have asked for me by name, and one other time old R—— was gracious enough to allow me to lead proceedings. On those earlier occasions I walked solemnly to the house in question and made arrangements with the grieving family of the deceased. I do well at my work, Liv. I would wish you to know that.

This morning the circumstances were altogether different. I was informed that a cadaver had been discovered and that my presence had been requested to oversee its retrieval. Retrieval! The phrase made my skin prickle, and yet I maintained a brave countenance as I bade frail R—— farewell, directed our stable boy to prepare carriage and horses, and set off after the constables.

Our destination was the public park at the riverside—or rather, the pathway that runs alongside the park, directly at the water's edge. A crowd had already formed at the railings, but uniformed men held the masses at bay, restraining the onlookers admirably whilst still each retaining a free hand to touch their fingers to their caps as I approached. The route they desired me to take, it became evident, was through a narrow parting in the railings. I tore my cloak as I squeezed through the gap and I am ashamed to confess that I swore.

Beneath the railings runs a sluice from the park to the mud bank of the river. Only three nights ago heavy rains flooded the park, undoing all of the planting and sweeping away the Autumn leaf-carpet overnight. The sluice has belched with water thereafter. Within the park grounds, though inaccessible from the mown stretches of the park proper due to foliage thicker than the blackness of night, is a gully that feeds the sluice. It was in this gully that the constables directed me to observe a body.

I stood on the filthy bank of the gully, my arms acting as windmills to prevent my slipping down the slope, and I stared at the figure lying there below me.

And Olivia— I laughed.

The amazement of the constables made the laughter die in my throat, and soon I displayed my own amazement when I saw their wide eyes and their horror.

I pointed down into the gully at the lifeless figure.

—But you joke, said I. It is a puppet!

Two of the constables had already clambered into the gulley and stood at the head and toes of the enormous doll. They turned and gazed up at me and then down again at the wooden effigy.

—Will you or will you not provide transport to your premises? the man beside me enquired.

I maintained that of course I would not. To make a mockery of an undertaker's role would be dreadful enough even without consideration of the repercussions upon my own reputation.

A fight of words ensued but, even as we fought, the body was being raised from its bed—with such care and gentleness that I broke off at moments to laugh again at the sight of so many men acting as fools over a toy. And yet they were as serious about their business as if this were a real cadaver rather than—as I saw plainly now—a huge thing made of wooden struts polished and unvarnished. Even more strange, the men then cast down a rough blanket and laid the puppet upon it, then set to the task of carrying it to the railings, whereupon the crowd of onlookers gasped as one and stepped back, terror evident in all their expressions. With much consternation and huffing, constables on either side of the railings eased the doll through the railings, their lips curled with distaste and their heads turned aside as they stretched out their arms, as if the mere thought of touching the wooden surface of the figure was repellent. Once upon the pathway, together they lifted the doll onto my carriage. I began making amazed protestations, but my speech was cut short when I spied the look on our stable boy's face as he regarded the body within its blanket shroud and he wept.

I would not climb into the carriage. Instead I walked behind it, back to my premises, with not the solemn pace of the undertaker but the wavering trudge of a dazed somnambulist.

When we arrived, old R—— emerged from his rooms to observe the cadaver and to my further consternation—I had hoped to find in him common reasoning and the refutation of this vile prank—his pallor whitened and he gripped the table and whispered: I knew him!

At this, I confess, my certainty fell away. I approached the table and regarded the thing, as my mentor and the stable boy wept at either side of me. But the cadaver was no man! The effigy was wooden throughout, and it was no devious construction. Despite the grime transferred from the gulley I could see plainly the pins that had been driven into the upper parts of the spindle legs and through the shoulders. Its face was a blank surface, barely rounded at all, more of the appearance of a blunt shoe-horn than any mortal's visage.

I lifted one of its arms. The shoulder-pin squealed and at this R—— leapt upon me, enraged, forcing me away so that the puppet's limb dropped to the table once more with a dull sound like a knock upon a door.

Thereafter, R—— in a quiet fury insisted that I stand apart from proceedings while he tended to the body, as he put it. And yet, Liv, he did nothing of the sort! Had he produced a chisel or sandpaper I would at least have appreciated that his methods matched this waking dream, but he neither did this nor did he work in the normal manner. Even so, it was several hours before he pronounced his ministrations complete, whereupon I watched mutely as a procession of townsfolk entered the room and wept over the effigy—women wailing and men pressing their lips tight together as they looked upon the wooden abomination and then clapping one another upon the shoulders as they departed.

To-morrow morning I am to deliver the body—as I am compelled to call it—to the church, and then the gravediggers will be watched on by a priest as the effigy is interred in sacred ground. And here lies my principal uncertainty. Can I allow this to pass, Olivia? If all the people of G—— suffer from a shared dream, or perhaps a nightmare, is it a necessity that I follow suit though I see the truth of the matter? Surely that cannot be the case, particularly when it is God himself who is being mocked by this burial.

But there is another, deeper, fear. What if they are all correct in their vision and I am wrong? What if beyond this crossroads, or milestone, or borderline, only madness awaits, or what if I have already begun the walk along that path?

Liv— I do not know what to ask of you. By the time you receive this letter I will already have cast the dice. No; there is something I can ask. Will you pray for me?

Yours forever,

And there it ends, Will, just as I have ended it, unsigned. I'd love to know what you make of it all.

But the letter itself wasn't the source of my initial shock. As I finished reading I looked up at the window behind my desk, imagining the town of G—— and its 'belching' sluice containing the abominable doll. It was only just three o'clock but the skies had darkened during the hour I had been in my study, and the room was dim and eerie. And I appreciate that it is a cliché, but I saw a movement out of the corner of my eye. Not on the floor or near the door, but to the left of my field of vision, on the bookcase.

You may remember my idiosyncratic, and very slim, collection of essays on Poe that was published a decade or so ago. You may not remember that, in a fit of uncharacteristic confidence, I produced miniature illustrations for each essay. Anyway, the important detail is that on the bookcase there stands the single item of artist's paraphernalia that I bought in preparation for the task: a small wooden mannequin with limbs capable of being angled and held in a variety of positions.

And believe me, I know how this sounds, Will, I swear I do – but the thing moved. I shook my head, maybe to clear it or maybe just a vigorous 'No', and swivelled my desk lamp to point up at the bookcase. My relief that I saw no further movement was short-lived. The phenomenon I experienced next was, presumably, due to the motion of the light playing upon the blank face of the mannequin. But there is no explanation for the particular vision I saw. On the blank surface of the mannequin's head I saw a human face, and one I recognised: Professor Ferdy Bruhl!

It's important to me that I write this all down, Will. It's important that I get the order of events right in my head.

Because then I was startled by something far more mundane: the ringing of the phone. You know I detest them, and I allowed one in the study only because of Marie's insistence in case I suffer the indignity of reaching the apex of old age by 'having a fall'. So I let it ring on, each trill jangling my nerves, until Marie answered elsewhere. I stared at the mannequin, then looked down at my hands, then recoiled as I saw that the letter-paper had stained my fingertips yellow and, worse still, the paper itself was already degraded so badly that I could barely read the words.

The order of events is important, because it was soon *after* this that Marie entered my study to tell me the sad news that Professor Bruhl, though he had lived a full, long life and enjoyed an acclaimed career, was dead.

I'm sorry to pass this news on to you, Will, and in such a roundabout manner. I know you'll raise a glass tonight – whenever you receive this letter, anyway – to our erstwhile tutor. Eighty-nine is a fine age. And if I know you at all, and if you remain more or less the same Will that you were when we lived only a few doors apart, I think you will appreciate the macabre flavour of my experience.

Yours,

# |Four Fabrications of Francine Descartes|

~

With another day comes another boarding of a ship. Other captains may prefer to oversee proceedings from afar, but I have always dirtied my hands. I roll and stow barrels, I tug and test riggings. Yet my duties are doubled. Alongside the preparedness of the ship, I watch for signs of anything human that may be amiss. I do not mistake my crew for friends, nor family. But together they form a living organism, and that organism in its totality may be hearty or it may fall prey to illness.

Today the crew are merry and perform their work diligently, as if they run on tracks and have no sway over their actions. The *Fortuin* is crammed with goods. Perhaps it is only their transportation from Amsterdam that should be my concern, and yet if a single produce were to be named I could lead a person with great confidence to a particular shelf at a particular level of the hold. The ship is more than my livelihood. It is my mind, external to my skull.

The few passengers arrive last, slipping into the gaps that remain after our careful work of loading. I wish that we were not compelled to carry passengers. They are the sand in the workings of the clock.

I stand at the head of the gangway and shake each of their hands in turn. I bow my head and describe myself as their servant. Most nod respectfully. Those who fail to do so warrant being watched – they are the ones who believe I really am their servant, who assume that they may dictate the operation of the ship and that on this crossing I will be their hands.

There are twelve passengers in all. A family of seven, being moved wholesale to Sweden by a diplomat paterfamilias. Two spinster women whose cheeks inflame when they address me. A trader and his man who intend to seek new fortune after finding only failure and bankruptcy in Holland. And there is one other man, with a large nose and sardonic eyes, who is followed by two of my crew hauling a box.

By now I find it an almost automatic process, the determination of which piece of grit presents the greatest threat to the workings of my machine.

We labour, my men and I. At their sides I work the ropes, the sails, as well as issuing orders. It is my role to be everywhere and to see everything. The crossing is due to take three days, during which time I will sleep for seven or eight hours in all.

I make myself available to the passengers, by which I mean that I show my face and I reassure them that the severe rocking of the vessel is usual, that our forecasts will hold, that their seasickness will pass, that all is safe. Eleven of the passengers listen attentively to all I say, and they are eager to know that they will reach Gothenburg to continue their lives according to their own plans.

The man with the wooden box and little other luggage nods curtly and does not permit me to cross the threshold of his room. He asks me no questions, so I ask my own. He replies that he is a writer, a thinker, and that he has been summoned to Stockholm by none other than Queen Christina. She is building an 'Athens of the North', a scientific academy, and he is to tutor her in, of all things, *love*. Evidently, Mr René Descartes is an important man.

After closing the door I pause, absorbing all that I have been told. I am an intelligent man, with wits perhaps beyond my station, and the information provided by Descartes has set something moving in my mind. There is a world beyond the practical, a world of thought and ideas. It is seductive. But it would be wrong to barrage a passenger with questions. The model that dictates the successful operation of this ship would not allow for it. I begin to move away from the door – but then I stop again at the sound of voices. One belongs to Descartes. The other is the voice of a young girl.

No captain can know the organism of a ship, or the intricacy of its operation, perfectly. Any organism, any model, contains imperfections. It is appropriate that on the *Fortuin* these imperfections are leaks, though they are leaks that take the form of talk rather than the ingress of the sea. I know I will never determine the pathways by which rumours of Descartes' box reach my crew.

The allegations vary wildly. I dismiss them all. Yet my crew chew on rumour as they chew on salt beef; it is a lazily pleasurable occupation while the body is hard at work.

The voice of the girl is common to all the tales.

I find myself returning to Descartes' door, my ear pressed against the wood. I listen to the murmurs from within. The girl's tone is clearer than Descartes' muttering; it is bright like a bell. She calls him Papa.

Until late on the second day the conditions of our passage are straightforward. I and my crew operate almost without conscious thought, so familiar has our route become. From Amsterdam we sail to the island of Texel, and then there is a short wait for high tide. Ships are frequently wrecked on this path – warships, grain ships and whalers – but the pride of the merchant vessels of the East India Company will not permit such accidents to occur. Then we travel past the West Frisian Islands to enter the shallow Wadden Sea, a cursed region for any captain who does not appreciate the cruelty of a lowering tide, more treacherous than any storm.

Perhaps that is why a real storm takes us by surprise. I should say that it takes *me* by surprise, because I am the eyes and the mind of the *Fortuin*.

The aft bears the first shock. I am at the bow, gazing mute into the black clouds that for hours have been pregnant but which now birth their flood. I swing about to see the bulge as the first deck fills, then the great cabin bursts. I roar at the crew but they are already scampering, skidding on the glistening deck, heaving at ropes without clear purpose. The organism is already suffering, the machine is already broken.

All my responsibilities of the past amount to nothing. Hierarchies of rescue leap unbidden to my mind. In the frenzy I cannot account for all of my crewmen. I rush to the rowing boats lashed to the side of the ship. Only one is there. The other has either been torn away by the water, or it has been taken already.

The crew's purpose has listed out of alignment, along with the ship. They pay no attention to the sails or ropes. Some of them emerge antlike from below decks, pushing empty barrels before them. They mean to escape and survive.

I may be the head of this ship, but I am at the lowest end of its hierarchy. I am not fool enough to hope to go down with the *Fortuin*, but I will be damned if I am not the last on board. I rush from cabin to cabin, raising the alarm as if my passengers were not already aware that catastrophe has struck. The sons of the diplomat are pulling their parents from their room, pleading with them to abandon their possessions in favour of their lives. The eyes of the two spinster women are wider than ever. The trader's man is puking violently and the trader himself has already climbed from the window of his room and is gone.

When I push open the door of his room, René Descartes raises his head to observe me. He is calm and still.

Come, I tell him. You must all flee.

He does not rise from his sitting place at the foot of his bed.

As one, we turn to look at his box. The lid is awry, and it strikes me that despite the lurching of the ship this is the only evidence of disturbance within the room.

She must come too, I say.

Descartes places a hand on the lid of the box.

I will be damned if am not the last on board. I push Descartes aside and pull away the lid.

Immediately, a shape rises up, as though the figure is hinged at the waist. Her hair is fair. She wears a plain smock. Her face is painted wood and her eyes are beads. Her hands lift jerkily towards me. It is a vision from a nightmare, but at this moment everything is.

Even if it is only Descartes that is mortal and must be saved, in his leaping to his feet he has illustrated that he dotes upon the girl, whatever she may be. He will follow her. I snatch her up – she is heavier than I anticipated, her mass unevenly distributed – and rush from the room. I hear Descartes in my wake, calling after me, but I do not stop.

Upon the deck I am met with a tempest. Nothing is visible but streaks of chaos. I rely upon the memory of my limbs to navigate to the winch above the single rowing boat, which is already partway descended to the roiling sea. Lightning flashes reveal figures, but whether they are crew or passengers, I cannot tell.

Descartes pulls at my arm, trying to free the wooden girl. I knock him aside, then take advantage of his imbalance, shoving him so that he staggers from the deck and drops into the boat. He twists to look up at me, his mouth contorted in a blind shout.

Then catch her, I yell.

I shift the girl from my shoulder and hold her before me. Her face is slack but her jaw works and words come forth, though they are no louder than whispers amid the crashing thunder.

As she falls, she strikes the edge of the rowing boat. I swallow bile, telling myself that she is only luggage. Her torso shatters at the same moment the bow of the *Fortuin* shatters. I shield my eyes from the splinters.

Somehow, the voice of René Descartes reaches my ears.

From far below he bellows, Again!

With another day comes another boarding of a ship. Other captains may prefer to oversee proceedings from afar, but I have always dirtied my hands. I roll and stow barrels, I tug and test riggings. I shout at my crew, who like children understand only the assertion of authority.

The crew are merry and perform their work diligently. I will reward them with biscuits, like dogs.

The few passengers arrive last. I wish that we were not compelled to carry them. They are sand in the creases of my palms, producing calluses.

I stand at the head of the gangway and shake each of their hands in turn. I say nothing, waiting for their bows of respect.

There are twelve passengers in all. A family of seven, being moved wholesale to Sweden by a diplomat paterfamilias. Two spinster women whose cheeks inflame when they address me. A trader and his man who intend to seek new fortune after finding only failure and bankruptcy in Holland. And there is one other man, with a large nose and sardonic eyes, who is followed by two of my crew hauling a box.

My men labour, and I watch them. It is my role to be everywhere and to see everything. The crossing is due to take three days, during which time I will sleep for seven or eight hours in all.

I have no interest in the passengers, yet I visit their quarters in response to a plea from the diplomat, whose wife is ill. I tell him there is nothing I can do for her, and that she must draw on her reserves and survive until we reach Gothenburg. I wish that they were mute, like the cargo in the hold.

On my return to the deck I pass the door of the man with the box, René Descartes. Voices come from within – his, and a young girl's. There are no young women aboard; the diplomat's children are all boys.

I throw open the door.

Descartes is sitting at the foot of the bed. The chamber is narrow enough that his feet touch the wooden box that has been placed beside it. Its lid has been pushed aside to reveal an interior filled with pillows and blankets. A girl sits upon the pillows, gazing up at him.

At once I see that she is made of wood. Her face is unpainted and crude. Her hair is a mass of strips of cotton. If it were not for her plain gown and the voice that comes from her snapping jaw, she would not be identifiable as a facsimile of a girl at all, but only a shade of indistinct human form.

Descartes turns to me. She is no threat, he says.

What is she?

My daughter.

I shake my head. I move towards the apparition. Through gaps in her cheeks I see machinery at work: metal gears and pinions.

I say, If my crew see her, they will not tolerate her being on aboard.

Then do not tell them.

You call her your daughter. Are you mad?

Descartes' head bows. Perhaps, yes. I did have a daughter. Francine. She died of scarlet fever at the age of five. If she had lived, she would be fourteen.

I look at the girl. Yes, her form is that of an adolescent.

You made her?

Do we not all make our children?

I move towards the girl.

No, do not touch her, Descartes says sharply.

I step back, but I keep watching the girl. Her movements are precise yet fluid. I am as attracted by the finery of the machine as I am repelled by her uncanny aspect.

You must keep her silent, I say. My crew will not abide her.

Afterwards my thoughts are filled with Francine Descartes, and so the storm takes me by surprise.

I roar at my crew, who yelp at my anger and at the anger of the storm.

It is not long before it is clear to me that the *Fortuin* cannot survive. Its workings are being stripped away by indiscriminate squalls.

I rush to the cabins, throwing passengers behind me and towards the lifeboats. If I survive, I intend to work again. Yet my true ambition is to reach Francine Descartes.

I find her in an embrace with her father. The sight produces within me a swell of envy. I stagger drunkenly into the chamber.

Save her, Descartes begs. She is proof that the corporeal body operates like a machine. Do not cast her into the sea.

I would not. I say it again: I would not. I never did.

Descartes frowns. What do you mean by that?

I would not endanger this machine, this girl. What will happen to her is not my doing.

I wrest Francine from him. He holds onto her left hand, tugging the fingers until some burst free.

She is lighter than I imagined. I carry her from the cabins to the deck. The storm has amplified and the sky is filled with white knives.

The passengers throw themselves into the two rowing boats. Only Descartes stays behind. He holds out his arms.

Give me Francine.

I will not. Go now.

Overcome your ignorance, he says. Do not destroy her.

I watch my crew drop into the bellies of the lowering boats. You misunderstand me, I say. I have no wish to destroy her. I will die upon this deck. I will be damned if I will be alone.

With a firm grip on the wooden girl, I push Descartes over the edge and into the nearest boat. As he falls, he shouts, Again!

With another day comes another boarding of a ship. While my crew roll and stow barrels, tug and test riggings, I wait for René Descartes. He arrives, finally, with his box in tow. From my hiding place outside his door, I hear voices.

After we embark it requires subterfuge to draw Descartes from his cabin, where he has always taken his meals. He ought to wonder how Queen Christine of Sweden might send a message to a ship in the midst of the Wadden Sea, but Descartes' is a mind far from occupied with practical matters.

In his chamber, I prise away the lid of the unguarded box.

A girl lies within it on a bed of soft pillows.

She rises slowly and uncertainly, as though I have woken her. The skin of her face is golden.

You are not as I imagined you, I say in a hoarse voice.

What did you imagine, Captain Bastiaenszoon?

You know my name.

I know all.

No, I say. You are a complex machine.

Look at me, Francine says. Tell me whether or not I am a machine.

I stand back. Her white gown is turned golden by the glow of her skin. Her eyes vary from crimson to copper, like embers.

I do not know what you are, I say.

I am a salamander. A spirit of fire.

A sylph?

If you like.

I shake my head and mutter, This is not right. I am to see inside the box, and to see that you are an automaton made by Descartes in the image of his daughter.

She laughs. Did he tell you yet that I was named after the Francini brothers, who created the automata that reside within a cave at the royal chateau of Saint-Germain-en-Lay?

I frown. No. Not yet.

He did not make me, Francine says. I am not his daughter. I am his love.

His… love?

Would you prefer that I be yours?

Her radiance grows more intense. I shield my eyes. I do not answer.

You may place your hand on my cheek if you like.

Is this a trick?

You may be the judge, afterwards.

Hesitantly, I do as she bids. Her skin does not burn but the warmth is like no warmth I have experienced before. It travels along my arm, fizzing pleasurably as it goes.

I do not understand, I say. I do not understand you at all.

You are ignorant.

I consider this. Yes, of course. Of course I am ignorant of salamanders and sylphs.

Will you cast me overboard?

Why would I?

Because you fear me.

I hesitate. But why would I want to destroy you, simply because you are obscure?

Because that is what the ignorant do. It is what you do in this tale.

A crash sounds somewhere overhead. Francine's eyes rise to the ceiling and she smirks.

You know what that is? she asks me.

It is the storm, I say. It is always the storm.

She reaches out her arms. I suppose you will carry me to the deck now.

What would be the use of that? I reply. The ship is lost. I can do nothing to prevent it. I am as much use staying here with you as I can be up there. The *Fortuin* will operate just as well without me.

Her arms are still outstretched. I move into her embrace.

Again? she murmurs.

If we must, I reply.

With another day would come another boarding of a ship, if I had not ordered my crew to leave. They serve no purpose now, wandering the streets of Amsterdam in search of alternative occupation or pleasure, or perhaps they have simply been snuffed out. No barrels are rolled and stowed, no riggings are tugged and tested.

Yet René Descartes arrives on schedule, his box floating behind him for lack of crewmen to carry it.

Let us dispense with the trappings of this fantasy, I say.

He blinks in surprise. Then he sighs and nods. The box follows us to the deck, where we sit on chairs put there for the purpose. The box settles between us. I tap its lid.

What is she this time? I ask.

I do not know.

But this is your doing. Each of these scenarios is conjured by you.

Not exactly.

Are you truly René Descartes?

Out there? No.

I do not know what to make of his answer. I say, Conjured is the right word, is it not? It is a trick.

Yes.

For what purpose?

An experiment.

Is Francine the subject?

Descartes does not reply. He is watching me closely.

I bend to the box and prise the lid free. Its interior is filled with pillows and blankets. Upon them is a small black chest the size of a fist.

Is this Francine?

Descartes ignores me. He speaks to the black chest: Francine, my dear.

Yes, father? The voice that comes from the box is a girl's voice, bright as a bell.

Captain Bastiaenszoon would like to make your acquaintance.

Hello, Captain Bastiaenszoon. I'm very pleased to meet you.

Wonderingly, I reach into the wooden box and pick up Francine. The black chest trembles very slightly in my palm.

I am pleased to meet you too, Francine, I say. And it is true.

How may I help you today?

I frown. Why would you help me?

I like to help.

What are you?

I am an artificially intelligent personal assistant.

I know all of those words. But together they mean nothing to me.

I cower at the first flash of lightning. The storm has found us, despite the fact that we have not left Amsterdam. The *Fortuin* rocks wildly. Lashing rain obscures any glimpse of the docks. I will die here as readily as I have died at sea.

Descartes does not acknowledge the storm. Are you afraid? he asks.

Of course I am.

Of what?

Of the storm.

But not of Francine?

I look at the box in my hand. Why would I be afraid of her?

It is Francine who answers my question. Because you are ignorant.

It does not seem an insult, yet I feel obliged to put her right. I say, I may be ignorant – of automatons and spirits and artificial minds – but fear is another matter. Are you a threat?

I am more intelligent than you.

I have no doubt of that. Can you lash a rope to a mast?

No. But I am capable of charting safer courses than you or your navigator.

Then he and I will put our minds to other matters.

I confess that you surprise me yet again, Descartes says. I had supposed that you would rebel instinctively against change. Throughout history, it is the case that the ignorant have behaved in such a manner. Take Albertus Magnus—

I laugh. Albertus Magnus and his android capable of speech, which was destroyed by his student for interrupting his thoughts?

You are well informed, Captain.

It is a myth. It is no more real than… I look at the dark sky, then at the black box still held in my palm. It is no more real than this tale you are telling now.

Then I say, Francine, did René Descartes have a daughter?

She replies instantly. It appears that he did. Francine Descartes may have been the illegitimate child of René Descartes and a domestic servant, Helena Jans van der Strom. She died from scarlet fever aged five.

And did he build an automaton in her image?

There are varying accounts of this having occurred, all apocryphal.

My eyes raise to Descartes, who is shifting uncomfortably in his chair.

There are many more examples from more recent history, he begins. The Luddites—

I interrupt him. They desired only fair pay. They did not destroy the machines of factory owners who paid their workers fairly. That was a matter of economic justice, not ignorance.

You ought to know nothing about them, Descartes says weakly. They are centuries from now. Clearly, this model is imperfect.

All models are. All organisms are.

Not Francine. She is perfect.

Nonsense, I retort. Her perfection is only in comparison to lesser models.

I look up at the sky once more. The rain is formed of continuous white smears. The clouds are black cubes.

Lesser models.

All of it. The entire organism. The entire machine.

What is this experiment? I demand.

A test of ignorance.

I am the subject, then.

Naturally. And you have surprised at every turn. You must be congratulated.

With each of his pronouncements, the black chest shudders faintly.

It is you who answers my questions, I say to him. It is you who watches me. But this experiment is not yours. Is it? You are but an observer.

Descartes does not reply.

My hand that holds Francine is laced with scars earned during countless voyages. I want to believe that my face is similarly marked, though now it occurs to me that I have no knowledge of my appearance beyond my hands and the impression of a body at my core. I have no confidence that I have ever crossed the Wadden Sea.

I am a poor facsimile. I am no sailor, no captain. If this is a test of ignorance, it is imperfect as the test of the ignorance of man. Nevertheless, despite his fear and wonder and, yes, his ignorance, Captain Bastiaenszoon has not cast Francine Descartes from the ship in a storm, as the tale dictates.

Descartes continues watching me closely. The black chest hums.

You have won, I spit. Despite the growls of thunder my voice is loud, even if it is not bright like a bell. You have won, because now I am truly afraid.

I stand, knocking away my chair.

I shout, But know that it is not the fear of Captain Bastiaenszoon! You have underestimated him. I fear Francine, but mine is only the fear of a lesser model.

Descartes rises. He lurches towards me, his lips parting. I do not let him speak.

No! I bellow. Never again!

Before he can reach me, I throw Francine Descartes to the deck and I crush her beneath my boot.

# |Milk-White|

~

Full of life. That's how I am often described. Sometimes I believe it myself.

On those days, I flow through the palace like fluid. At each corner of each passageway I pirouette. I am all gratuitous motion. My hair spills behind me, my robe forms eddies in my wake.

None of this signifies happiness, exactly. Merely a thrill at my body.

Other days, I am inert. I lie in bed, unable to rouse myself, unable to lift a single limb, let alone dance. The physician has told my husband not to worry when I am like that. I am still alive and alert, he says. I am still real.

Which type of day is today?

I am up and out of bed. A great relief.

I eat sweet grapes, savouring each one, bursting them with carefully increased pressure of the tongue so that the flavour washes around my mouth and into my throat. Flavour is good, but motion is better.

I flow through the palace on a deliberate course. There are maidservants hidden around the building. They do their work and I do mine. They keep themselves away from me. Is that because they fear my wrath, or simply because they find me unnerving? If so, it is only likewise. Whenever one of them appears in a corridor, inertia slinks upon me from the feet up.

But today is a good day. My body is supple.

In the central atrium I greet the caged birds with a song of my own. My hand rests on the clasp of the cage. But if I set them free, there will be trouble. I dance away.

I've always been here.

It is surprising how a day can pass with nothing in it. I eat, I dance, I watch the street below the balcony. I can imagine how an artist might hope to capture the life of a scene such as this. The sun hangs high above and then begins to drop.

Somebody is singing, within the palace. I move to the door of my chambers.

I stop. It is discordant. It's no song at all.

I return to the balcony, but now the sound is impossible to ignore. It is louder than the chatter in the streets, louder than the calls from the marketplace, louder and more strident than the birds wheeling overhead. Louder than the sun which, as it sinks, shouts, "It is nearly time!"

I hurry from my room. I shout, too.

Where are the servants? This is their business, to prevent the shouts and screams.

They are nowhere. Perhaps they have fled the palace, fluid as I am, rushing out from its doors in a great stream, a waterfall tumbling into the city.

Perhaps I am alone here.

With the child.

My body moves towards it, in spite of my bidding. I could not have told anybody how to reach its room, but my feet know.

It is so *loud*. A palace is not large enough. I could never get far enough away.

I reach its chambers. The sound forms blades that slice me. My milk-white skin is lacerated.

It lies on a bed surrounded by railings. Unlike the cages of the birds in the atrium, there is no roof to keep it captive. Yet the child will never fly away.

There is another person in the room. Her body is bent over the railings, her arm upon the child. A rash act, it seems to me.

The child still shouts. The sound is like the shearing of cliffs. It strikes me in the belly again and again.

"Make it stop!" I cry.

Only now does the maidservant turn to see me. Her eyes are wide.

Hesitantly, she says, "Perhaps you would like to try?"

I watch her carefully. What might signs of loathing be? Her face is open and pleasant.

"Not today," I say.

She studies me for a moment longer, her lips parted. Then she turns and makes soothing sounds, touching the child. With each graze of her fingertips, I wonder if she will cut herself.

"You should go to your child," a deep voice says behind me.

I do not turn. Neither do I say, "Never."

"My lord," I say. It is a useful phrase, displaying obedience without specificity.

My husband passes me to enter the chamber. I watch his shoulders marked with plaster and dust, evidence that he has been at work in his studio all day. The maidservant backs away warily, though she is still making her soothing, hushing sounds. Perhaps she is unable to prevent it, a deflating sack of air.

Pygmalion smiles at her. Is she among his favoured ones? No. Her skin is not milk-white like mine.

"Let me," he says.

His short arms reach over the railings. As his stubby fingers touch the surface of the child, they produce squeaks that make me wince.

"My own child, my own child," he murmurs.

He raises it and turns to me. He grimaces; it's the closest he can come to a smile. His stub nose wrinkles. It is not for nothing that in my thoughts I call him the Pyg.

He is strong. He supports the child as if its mass causes him no trouble. Its sharp edges press into the skin of his arms and into his cheek where he has brought it to his face, but he makes no complaint. He kisses its broadest face and yet his lips do not turn blue with the cold.

It ought to inspire laughter, to see a man holding a great block of marble and treating it as something mortal. I glance at the maidservant, whose hands are clasped before her. She has stopped deflating and now she only watches the Pyg and his white marble block. Her head is tilted to one side in curiosity or adoration.

"Now you," the Pyg says, offering the child to me.

～

The marketplace is full to bursting. The pressure within the space is immense. Beyond the stalls in all directions I perceive breachable banks, and I imagine them failing, at which point everybody will spill from the square and down the hillside. What a joy that would be, such rapid movement! How I would love to be one among many, a mere particle in a mad dash to the sea.

The child would be left behind, of course. It would be far too heavy to be swept along.

My back aches. When I refused to take the child in my arms, the Pyg hurried away. When he returned he held in his hands the contraption I now wear. Harnesses and leather straps; bondage with a dual purpose.

The child is enclosed tightly within the straps, and it hangs before me. My hands are free, but my fears are greater than if I were touching the marble. Already the leather straps show signs of chafing. The sharp edges of the marble block will surely wear away at them. Then the child will simply drop, perhaps upon my toes, unprotected by my sandals.

I have few provisions to buy. The errand that the Pyg has set me is only for show. His intention is only to shame me.

All eyes are upon me.

And upon the child, of course. The people of the city have never known such a sight, a block of stone treated like a living thing.

The sellers behind their stalls are courteous and offer what I need. When they pass me the wares, I raise my hands, showing them my palms. They nod hurriedly and assure me that their boy will bring the goods to the palace. Before long I have a train of boys behind me, laden just as I am.

I have played my part, and my shoulders are screaming. At least the child has not woken. Any motion within the harness would be unbearable.

There is a huddle of women at the entrance to the marketplace. I form a new tributary, leading my boys. But when I emerge from the maze of stalls, the women are still somehow ahead.

One of them is the Pyg's sister. She waves.

I wave, and keep flowing with the current.

My gesture is not enough. Elishat flags me down as if I am a pack horse, which I suppose I may as well be.

Elishat's grimace is precisely the same as the Pyg's. She is a gruesome object.

"Dear, dear Galatea!" she sings. Her friends nod at her inane rhyme. "How wonderful to see you out in the open air! And it is even more wonderful for your delightful companion."

I turn to look at a boy standing directly behind me, who blushes.

Elishat steals closer to me. She points at the marble block. She taps her fingernails on it, then presses her cheek against its flat face. I shudder.

"An angel," Elishat says as she moves away. "An angel in slumber."

Her two friends surround me, staring up at me with open mouths, as though I am a public object on display: a fountain, or a... My heart quickens. No. Don't think of that.

"The stories of the child's beauty are quite correct," one of the women says.

"That milk-white skin!" another says.

Elishat smirks. "It is foretold that the child will be the foundation of the new city, which will be honoured with the name Paphos. Is that not so, Galatea?"

Bile rises up in my throat. It burns, but I relish it. It proves I'm not what they all say I am. I've always been here.

"So my husband tells me," I say.

I picture the child at a time when it has fulfilled the prophecy, when it has become the foundation stone of the new city. Trapped beneath hundreds of other marble blocks, perhaps thousands. Will I be forced to live in Paphos, cursed to listen to the howls of rage?

"I must go," I say. "My husband is entertaining friends tonight. I must prepare."

I do not prepare. That is what maidservants are for. I thrust the child into the arms of the first girl I encounter, and then I rush to my chamber and I drop onto the bed.

~

"Milk-White," a voice croons.

I do not respond. My throat is hard and could not produce sound even if I wanted to.

"Galat-e-a?" A song with no melody.

It is the Pyg. He should not enter my rooms. I would not venture into his chambers, or his studio, would I?

"You've slept for a very long time, Milk-White," he says. "I had supposed you were dressing."

I open my eyes. This small action elicits a murmur from somewhere in the room.

The Pyg stands at my bedside. He is no longer streaked in dust and there are no flakes of stone in his thick beard. He wears a robe of royal purple.

There are two other figures, at the foot of my bed.

"These are our guests," the Pyg says. "They would like to meet you." No.

"Galat-e-a! Your eyes have closed again."

There are more murmurs from the others, this time suggesting uncertainty.

"I assure you," the Pyg says, speaking to them and not to me, "she functions well. From time to time adjustments must be made, that's all. Return to the hall and enjoy your wine, and I will bring her out to you."

The pressure within the room lessens as they leave. I slip away, until the Pyg's stubby fingers dig into my shoulders. He lifts me to a sitting position, then turns me slowly so that my legs hang over the side of the bed.

"You need not go to any trouble," he says. "No adornments are necessary. A clean white robe would be most suitable."

The sounds from my throat are like those of the child. Stone against stone.

"I cannot," I say. "My body is stiff."

The Pyg pauses, then nods. "It is to be expected. Come with me."

He takes me by the hand and drags me from my room. My great weight is not enough to stop him.

I protest when I see where we are going. I have not been to the studio since… Perhaps I have never been there, despite what my husband says about me.

He pushes me through the doorway and onto a dais. He says "Stay there" and I do. He hums to himself as he arranges the tools he will require.

"My apologies for the delay," he says.

The men give reassurances, though they are weary and full of wine. One of them jeers and spills the contents of his cup on his chest. I've known men when they're like this, and they are not good.

"Finally," the Pyg says, "I present to you my milk-white Galatea."

This is my cue to appear. So I do. I sweep into the hall, fluid as ever.

I understand that there has been a transformation in me, but the effect is more pronounced than I expected. The men stop sipping from their cups. Their eyes are round, the pupils dancing as I dance.

I tell myself that I may neither take pride in nor feel shame at my actions. Even if the Pyg's tale about me is a lie, I have no choice.

It's clear that these men have never known a creature like me. It isn't a matter of appearances. My robe is as plain as those of the serving girls at the edge of the room. My hair is unbraided, my face unpainted. I appear to them as I was made.

One of the men stands. Clumsily, he places his cup on the floor.

"Where did you…" he breathes as he stumbles towards me.

I ebb away gracefully.

"Not *where*," the Pyg says. "You ought to ask *how*."

Another of the men rises from his seat. "She is from the temple, surely. I have seen the priestesses there. Though none quite like this."

I watch the familiar leer grow on my husband's face. "From the temple? In a sense. But I must take most of the credit, as the effect is impossible without the form."

"Enough riddles. Speak plainly, Pygmalion."

The Pyg nods.

"Spin," he says to me.

I spin.

"Faster," he says.

I spin faster.

"Faster still," he says.

Most would retch, but I do not. I spin faster.

"She is mine to command," the Pyg says.

Then he says, "I created her."

Then, "I carved her from stone in my studio."

As I spin, the faces of the guests are smeared, only the whites of their staring eyes visible.

"She was perfect when I made her," the Pyg continues, "as perfect as any statue could be. But that was not enough for me. I went to Aphrodite and made my case. And the goddess granted my wish."

I will make myself sick, spraying them all.

"Stop," the Pyg says.

I stop spinning. The faces before me are still smeared. Perhaps that it simply how they are.

"If you perceive her as grace, that is because she *is* grace," the Pyg says. "She is Galatea, my milk-white. Yet as good a name is Aphrodite, whose spirit infused the perfect form I carved."

The men all scoff. But they are still watching me.

"She is very fine," one says. I know it is an understatement.

"So very pale." He giggles. "Is she cold to the touch?"

"Not so cold as you might imagine," the Pyg says.

In a knowing tone: "I heard she has borne you a child?"

A nod.

"You dog. You once had a reputation as a celibate."

For the first time, the Pyg is hesitant. He considers his chasteness a matter of great pride. The idea has always been ludicrous. For all his railing against prostitution within the city, his employment of lowly *pornai* and higher-class *hetairai* has always been so frequent as to be impossible to disguise. His voice catches as he says, "Another of the goddess's miracles. Galatea bore me a child, and yet my milk-white remains as perfect as ever."

One of the men reaches out to me, but his fingers do not touch my skin. "This tale of a statue brought to life. Is it true?"

"I would not lie," the Pyg replies.

The guest shakes his head. "I am asking *her*."

I watch him. He is as piglike as the Pyg. All men are.

"Is it true?" he asks again. "Were you once stone, and were you brought alive by the spirit of Aphrodite?"

I do not reply.

The man turns to my husband. "Then does she not speak?"

"If so, that is another boon!" the other guest roars, but he is silenced with a glare.

"She speaks," the Pyg says. "She is perfect in every way. Galatea, tell our friends the truth."

My mouth opens obediently even before I have my answer.

"I am from the temple of Aphrodite," I say.

"Ha! That hardly supports your husband's tale."

"Galatea," the Pyg says. "Is it not true that you were once stone, carved by my own hand?"

"Yes," I say. A clever response. It is *not* true.

"And if I wish it," he continues, "you will return to stone?"

All my confidence floods from me. "Yes," I say, quieter.

"And all of your grace is a gift of the goddess Aphrodite?"

"Yes."

"Then show our guests your grace."

I show them.

Afterwards, I am brittle.

Is this how it is to be from now on? Until tonight, the Pyg has been intent on keeping me for himself. What has changed?

The child, I suppose. He has his foundation stone now. The city of Paphos will be his legacy.

I've always been here, and I have always been a prisoner. But even prisoners might be left alone, like the birds in their cages who sing merrily enough.

The Pyg has made more than one mistake tonight. If he had not taken me there to work upon me, I would never dare enter his studio.

I do not like cold things as a rule, but the metal chisel feels natural and good in the grip of my left hand. I do not always perceive strength in my body, but as I raise the mason's mallet in my right hand I am strong.

The child is sleeping. Just as well.

I breathe deep. Such a natural action, and it comes naturally to me. Because I am real.

I am *not* the Pyg's automaton. I am *not* a statue brought to life.

I've always been here.

Placing the chisel upon the sheer face of the marble block is enough to wake it.

Its shout is instantly unbearable. It is like the thunder of a mountainside tumbling.

I drop the chisel, the mallet.

Footsteps behind me.

"My lady!"

I do not turn. I cannot.

Instead, I stare at the child.

The marble block is *moving*.

Somehow, it rises to an upright position. How can it?

Its bellow is like the tearing of the ground in an earthquake.

It throws its arms above its head, reaching for me.

Wait—

—arms?

It has limbs. And a head. A pristine white face.

Its skin is milk-white all over.

It is real. It is not a thing of stone.

So my husband speaks the truth.

Again: "My lady!"

A maidservant rushes past me, to the child, which she lifts from the bed. Its fingers grasp. Its eyes are fixed on me.

Eyes.

My husband speaks the truth.

If that is the case…

Then it means…

My left arm is still outstretched, the fingers curled despite the chisel having been dropped. My right hand is raised, malletless. The cold that began in my hands now travels along my arms, blooming in my chest, and then in an instant it floods to every remaining part of me.

I will never move again.

The maidservant turns and gazes at me. Her eyes are wide.

I understand what she sees.

I am milk-white, all over.

# |The Cardboard Voice|

~

"Chocolate bourbons are the best I can rustle up at short notice," Julia said as she returned carrying a tray. She had placed twelve of the biscuits on a fine china plate, arranged like the markers on a clock face.

How smiled wistfully and patted his stomach. "I'm on a regime," he said. "None of the good stuff for me, and ten thousand steps a day to work off the calories I'm not even allowed to eat."

"On whose say-so?" Julia asked.

"It's a thirty-day challenge, on a forum." In response to Julia's quizzical expression, he added, "A sort of a club, with everyone egging each other on."

"It sounds like a mean-spirited club," she replied. She set the tray precariously on a footstool, and passed a cup and saucer to How. She took one of the biscuits and proceeded to separate its top part carefully, then scrape the chocolate fondant icing with her front teeth. She smacked her lips and then grinned to acknowledge her peculiarly childish habit. It was as if a much younger person were occupying her old body.

"So what do I call you?" she said. "You signed your message Lee, but on your programme you call yourself How."

"You've seen my show?"

"Old people can use the internet too, you know," she retorted. "I didn't much like it, though. A bit whizzy for my tastes."

He nodded. "Everyone calls me How. It's from my surname. My name's actually Lee Howie."

"All right. How."

He sipped his tea, which was weak. "Thank you so much for agreeing to meet with me, Julia."

"I was intrigued. Maybe we'll both learn something. So, you're an expert in… forgery, is that right?"

How wrinkled his nose. "In a sense, I suppose. A very modern version of forgery. I'm an expert in what are known as deepfakes."

"Hence the title of your programme. What was it? *Truly, Madly, Deepfake* – that's it."

How had long regretted the title, which had occurred to him when he was an entirely different person. Now the subject had become a serious matter.

"Doctoring photos, as I understand it?" Julia continued. "Like Stalin making 'unpersons' by removing them from photographs and from the official record. Orwell's ideas, brought grimly to life."

How blinked in surprise. "Well, yes. That's actually a really good early example. I'll be referring to it in my talk – the one I'm preparing at the moment. But all of that is just a prelude to the modern phenomenon. There are still plenty of doctored photos, but video is where it's at."

"You make it sound almost exciting."

"Well, yes." How leant forward in his armchair, which creaked under his weight. "I can't deny I find it fascinating. I wouldn't have dedicated myself to exposing deepfakes otherwise."

Julia polished off another biscuit at a leisurely speed. Why she remained so thin was a mystery.

"And yet, like Stalin, surely the most obvious applications are negative ones? People pretending to be other people… it hardly sounds like a development that's going to result in world peace."

How considered making a gesture towards the usual argument: that new technology was neither good nor bad, that any new development could be misused. But he sensed that Julia understood that already. She was far sharper and more engaged than he had anticipated.

"You're right," he said. "There'll be plenty of benign uses – bringing dead Hollywood stars back to life onscreen, broadcasting politicians' speeches in different languages, with them actually speaking those words. But yes, there'll be a swathe of negative uses too. I can't deny that's what I find morbidly fascinating."

"So… videos featuring those same politicians, apparently caught *in flagrante delicto*, resulting in an end to their careers. Famous people seeming to express wild viewpoints, and perhaps calling upon their adoring fans to perform radical actions. Respectable young women taking their clothes off. Am I close?"

"Very close. You're very well informed, or else very imaginative."

Julia waved a hand dismissively. "It's nothing new, only more convincing. You seem very confident in your videos, by the way. Less so in person."

"I suppose it's an onscreen persona. A façade."

She smiled. "And there you have it. We're all pretending, aren't we? Even without technology tinkering with our image."

How considered this. "And you, Julia – are you pretending too?"

She laughed, leant back in her chair, sipped at her tea. Her thin eyebrows rose and fell rapidly as she savoured the taste, and it occurred to How that this was a unique characteristic. There was more to fakery than a simple image – mannerisms were an equally identifiable characteristic.

"Oh yes," she replied cheerfully. "I've been faking it my whole life." She gestured at their surroundings: the two plush sofas and luxurious wing-backed armchairs forming a horseshoe shape, the art-deco lamps, the heavy, embroidered curtains that reduced the sunlight to meagre slivers despite it being midday. Then she looked down at herself; her Harris tweed skirt and her thin ankles. "None of this is *me*."

How cleared his throat. "So, shall we talk about something real? Your grandfather. I'm eager to hear the story."

She sighed and placed her cup onto its saucer.

"Grandad was a lovely fellow. Had us kids in hoots of laughter whenever we'd visit. Quite a dab hand at conjuring tricks, which is quite apt, isn't it? But of course you don't want to hear about his later life."

How offered a smile of encouragement.

Julia continued, "It was in 1931. Mid-February. Grandad, on behalf of the Producers Distributing Company, invited the four journalists to their London offices. Of course, they didn't call him Grandad, so neither should I when I'm telling this story. Eric Allan Humphriss – a grand name, isn't it? And yet I've always resented the surname attached to myself. Children in the playground called me 'Humpy' – and it was almost Grandad's undoing, too."

"In what way?"

"Sloppy fact-checking. When the story was reported, journalists kept spelling his name 'Humphries'. That's part of the reason I wanted to tell you the story: to avoid him being consigned to the dustbin of history. So, anyway, there's Eric, and there are the four journalists, in that office in London. Before starting work there, Eric had been an engineer at RCA, and had developed their wonderful Photophone technology. Have you heard of it?"

"I'm afraid not. I was never a film student."

She scoffed. "You don't need to be. It's just interesting, that's all. Anyway, what he invented was the ability to include the soundtrack to a film on the physical film itself. Talkies were in their very early days at the time, obviously, and synchronised sound was something of a holy grail. His clever idea removed any issues about starting the soundtrack for each reel at precisely the right moment. And of course the way he did it was to include an *image* of the sound. Just like you'd see nowadays. A... I'm not sure how you'd describe it."

"A waveform?" How ventured.

"Yes. Yes, a waveform. Or, to the untrained eye, a long blotch with wiggly tops and bottoms. And it worked wonderfully – any sound could be recorded and its shape captured on film, and then a projector could shine a light through that tiny strip of film and the amount of light getting through would reproduce the sound itself. Don't ask me how, though. Anyway, Eric didn't stop there. He was a perpetual inventor – you should have seen some of the toys he produced in his shed in later life! But back then, he realised that if a sound could be recorded and its shape contained on film, then it must be possible to create *new* shapes, and use those blotches to create entirely new sounds."

"And others did too, didn't they?" How said. "Composers created music by drawing shapes."

Julia nodded. "But like you, Grandad was fascinated by forgery. His obsession was to recreate the human voice. He worked and worked at it, studying the shapes of recorded voices, convincing himself that he could learn to read and produce all phonetic sounds in visual form. What a project!"

"And he achieved it? He demonstrated it to those journalists in 1931?"

Julia shrugged modestly, as though her grandfather's achievement were her own. "Near enough. He played the men a single phrase, which he had created from scratch as a result of his studies. And they were *dumbfounded*. I only wish I could have been there to see the looks on their faces."

How nodded eagerly. "And what was the phrase?"

Julie giggled, sounding more like a child than a septuagenarian. "He was a terrible joker, never behaving as you'd expect. But even so, I have no idea why he chose the words he did."

She watched How for several seconds, clearly enjoying the suspense.

"It was a deep male voice," she said. "The reports said it was as clear as a bell. And in this commanding tone it said, 'All… of… a… tremble…'"

How exhaled the breath he hadn't realised he'd been holding in. "All of a tremble?"

"All of a tremble. Goodness knows what was going through his mind. And to think he spent a hundred hours creating the shape."

"I'm sorry – what?" How exclaimed. "Did you say a hundred hours?"

"At least. Any good forger is prepared to put in the time." Her eyes gleamed. "Perhaps you don't appreciate how detailed it was. In order for the photograph on the film strip to capture all of the complexities of the human voice, Eric had to make it in ink at an enormous scale. Forty feet long!"

How puffed out his cheeks. "I had no idea. That's… that's incredible. I wish I could have seen it."

Julia's head tilted. "Well, I could show it to you."

How scrutinised her face. He imagined that there was a lot of Eric Allan in his granddaughter – the same love of tricks.

"You're teasing me, Mrs Robinson," he said.

Julia wrinkled her nose. "You won't want to accompany me to the barn, then?"

Julia's theatrical instinct remained evident; she threw open the doors of the barn with a flourish, startling a young man wearing a flat cap who had been in the process of sharpening a pair of shears on a grindstone (an act that How could scarcely believe anybody performed in the twenty-first century). Then, in a windowless room at the rear of the barn, she insisted that How remain on the blank side of the long sheet of cardboard as he unfolded its panels like a dressing-room screen. It took him several attempts to prop it on its end, Julia watching on and barking instructions like a foreman on a construction site, and How winced as the lower edge scuffed on the uneven concrete floor strewn with hay.

"All right," she said finally. "You can come around to this side now."

When he stood beside Julia, he put his hand over his mouth.

"It's beautiful," he whispered.

"D'you think so? I always thought it looked like a conga line of slugs."

He shook his head empathically, but didn't reply. The cardboard stretched the full length of the barn wall, and at first glance, the waveform upon it did appear like a series of traipsing hunched figures, though How saw them more as a herd of elephants with each tail held in the trunk of the one behind. However, that was only a fleeting impression. The swells were all of different sizes, their contours varying; some sloping steeply to a vertex, others bobbing uncertainly, others with fuzzed exteriors like caterpillars. What struck How was the sheer detail of the inked peaks, revealing the steadiness of the hand that had painstakingly described each shape in minute detail. The more How looked at it, the more he felt as if he were parachuting towards this inky mountain range which grew larger and larger, enveloping him.

How swallowed noisily. He wiped his eyes. "I'm sorry," he said. "I hadn't expected to be so moved by it."

She laughed softly. "Grandad would be delighted. Though, of course, it was never intended as an artwork. Perhaps he'd be downhearted at the idea of it becoming nothing more than a funny-looking painting."

"But that's not what it is at all," How said sharply. "It's a code, a key, as much as it ever was."

"If you had the right sort of projector, I suppose that's true. But I certainly don't have one. You'd have had your work cut out finding one any time after the war."

How stared at her. "But it's a *waveform*. It's universal – your grandfather would have known that, and understood he was creating something that would last beyond any fleeting technology."

"You mean—"

He nodded excitedly. "Hold on."

He pulled out his phone and tapped its screen. "There. It's the modern mantra, Julia: *there's an app for that*. Welcome to the twenty-first century."

He opened the app, then flipped his phone horizontal and stepped back so that the image onscreen encompassed the entirety of the waveform. Julia waited patiently as he cropped the resultant image to include only the cardboard strip.

Once finished, his finger remained hovering over the play button.

"Could we pop back indoors?" he said. "My phone speaker's rubbish. I feel we should pay enough respect to your grandfather's work to listen to it in decent quality."

Julia took his arm and they walked together back to the large house.

They were silent until How blurted, "Would you consider selling it to me?"

"It's an heirloom. And what would you do with it, anyway?"

"I honestly don't know. It's just that… I don't know. My line of work is all digital, all abstract. Coming across an honest-to-goodness artefact like this, a slice of history… it feels important, that's all."

"Then it'll be here waiting, whenever you need to be overwhelmed all over again."

In the sitting-room How fiddled with the leads behind the amplifier and then angled the heavy wooden speakers so that they pointed at the middle sofa, where Julia sat.

"Gentlemen," he said in something approximating a stage magician's tone. "What you will hear today is a marvel the likes of which have never been experienced before. I have studied this phenomenon to the point where I can read the physical shape of a voice as readily as if they were words in a book. Today, I am able to present to you the first synthetic voice – a voice that is not a voice, and words that had never been spoken."

He bowed his head to the screen of his phone connected to the amplifier. He clicked play.

From the speakers came a sonorous, deep voice.

*"All... of... a... tremble..."*

It spoke more slowly than How had expected, and despite the slight flattening which conveyed a nasal tone to the voice, as though the man had a slight cold, there was also a surprising suggestion of humour to the delivery. Only now did it occur to How that the voice may actually be Eric Allan Humphriss's own voice – or rather, an ink approximation of an image of a true recording of it.

Another oddity was the clicking sound in the background, rather like the scuffing of a record player's needle: three dull staccato clicks that triggered something in How's mind, an association that remained out of reach.

He looked up to see that Julia was dabbing at her eyes with a handkerchief.

"My word," she said. "Wasn't that something?"

"Would you like to hear it again?"

"No," she replied hastily. "No. Just the once. I'd rather it be a once-in-a-lifetime experience. You don't get those often, at my age. But thank you, How. Thank you so very much."

They continued chatting, but How found himself surreptitiously checking his phone, and it was clear that Julia was tired after her emotional experience. Soon, he made his excuses and insisted he would see himself out.

He turned in the doorway of the sitting-room. "I should fold up the cardboard strip again. And would you allow me to bring it into the house rather than leave it out there in the barn? The thought of it amongst all that straw gives me the shudders."

She nodded, her eyes shining.

He went immediately to the barn. Before he folded up the cardboard strip he gazed at it for several minutes. He could see no evidence in the meandering waveform of the three clicks he had heard.

Preparation for the TEDx talk occupied How entirely for several days. He paused only to record a new episode of *Truly, Madly, Deepfake* on the subject of Dr. Dre's 'duet' with a computer-generated, apparently three-dimensional 'hologrammatic' Tupac Shakur at the Coachella Festival in 2012 – in reality an application of the 'Pepper's Ghost' illusion first popularised 150 years earlier. But How felt his delivery seemed phoned in, and he struggled to maintain his screen persona despite the short running time. He was a different person now.

He didn't listen to Julia's waveform again, though he couldn't have explained why he was reluctant to do so.

"I think we're good," Gabrielle said, putting her camera on the coffee table in How's tiny apartment.

"You have enough shots in profile?" How asked. "They're just as important as front-facing ones, aren't they? Otherwise I won't be able to look left and right without introducing artifact blotches."

"Trust me," Gabrielle said. She tapped the camera. "I have enough images of you here to recreate you entirely, doing anything that may take my fancy. It's just as well you're a bloke, and an ugly bastard to boot. Anyone more attractive would be at perpetual risk of being inserted into porn vids shared on the internet. You should consider yourself lucky."

How snorted. "Talk about a back-handed compliment, Gab. And *you're* lucky that I trust you."

"You know, we could actually do that, you know…" Gabrielle said thoughtfully, rubbing her shaven head.

"Fake me into a porn clip?" How said, appalled.

"Yeah. I mean, wouldn't that be the most impactful demonstration during your talk? You'd be putting your money where your mouth is, highlighting the dangers of this new AI."

"Sure. But…"

He watched her carefully. Her expression appeared deadly serious. Then, gradually, a grin formed.

"I'm yanking your chain," she said, rocking back in her seat gleefully. "You think anyone'd hang around to watch if you subjected them to *that*?"

He exhaled with relief. "Plan A, then?"

"Plan A. Putting together your avatar will be easy enough. Then we'll rig up the kit that'll allow you to manipulate the image in real time. Have you decided who you want to morph into for the showstopper?"

How scratched his temple. "I'd have said Barack Obama, if it hadn't already been done. It has to be somebody who commands respect, somebody who'd never say what I'll make them say."

"Before you get carried away, let me remind you it also needs to be somebody who's appeared in loads of video footage," Gabrielle said. "Ideally against a plain background, to save me some work."

"A newsreader?"

"They'll say whatever's put on the teleprompter."

"Some pop star?"

She chuckled. "'Pop star'? Do you realise how out of date you sound, Mr Finger-on-Society's-Pulse?"

He crossed to the kitchenette. "I'll keep thinking of ideas. As for now, fancy a drink and bit of fooling around for old time's sake?"

Gabrielle smiled indulgently. "I'll take the drink, but then I'd better turn in. Mind if I kip here tonight? Solo – if that doesn't offend you."

How did his best to adopt an expression that suggested no offence taken. "You can have my bed," he said. "I'm not tired yet, and the sofa'll do me just fine."

~

He had no idea what time it was when he woke with a start. The apartment was as close to pitch black as it ever got, the dim neon of the fast-food restaurants across the street lending the room an eerie glow.

What had woken him?

A sound.

He replayed it in his mind, then shuddered.

Three dull staccato clicks, just like he had heard on the waveform playback.

He reached up and fumbled for the light switch, then winced at the resulting brightness.

Then he stood to face the clock on the wall to his right.

It had once belonged to his father, an object so familiar that he barely even registered its presence. Now that he examined it properly, it seemed absurd, with its twee cottage roof and the little red hatchway above the clock face.

The cuckoo had never emerged from its housing, though How knew it was in there; he'd once levered the hatch open with a screwdriver. There was something wrong with the mechanism, and he'd never attempted to fix it.

According to the clock, it was one minute after three.

His hand trembled slightly as he nudged the minute hand backwards. The red hatchway shook a little with each click in place of a chime. Three dull clicks, each with a slightly delayed echo as the cuckoo struck the inside of the door.

The same sounds he had heard at Julia's house.

It didn't make sense. He darted into the hallway and rummaged in his jacket pocket for his earbuds, then returned to the sofa. He opened the waveform app, brought up the image of Humphriss's ink picture, then hesitated for several seconds before clicking play.

"*All... of... a... tremble...*"

This time, the voice elicited entirely different responses. The flattened tone evoked both mean-spiritedness and an image of somebody calling via an old phone line, like a kidnapper conveying demands in a Hollywood thriller. The suggestion of humour How had identified now seemed like mockery.

And though the clicking sounds were *precisely* the same as the vain efforts of the trapped cuckoo… there were only two of them.

"Is that really what I look like?" How asked. "What I act like?"

The How on the computer screen mouthed the same questions, aping his movements in real time. How raised his right hand and waved, and after only a fractional lag as the motion was captured by the camera rig jerry-rigged in the centre of the lounge and then processed by the computer, the onscreen man waved too.

"'Fraid so," Gabrielle said. "You're a regular Frankenstein's monster."

How took a step forward so that his face was half a metre from the central camera. Looking out of the corner of his eye at the screen, he saw his face in close-up, eyes pointing to the left. It certainly was eerie, and he felt little connection with that person. But he had to admit that the detail was astounding. He could see the pockmarks on his face, and the skin on the bridge of his nose shone, and he saw the slight indents where his glasses had been pressing only minutes before. Only a slight rigidity to the lips, and a slight dullness in the eyes, gave the game away.

"Brace yourself," Gabrielle said.

He continued watching his doppelgänger as she knelt to tap commands into the computer keyboard resting on the coffee table.

Then, before he was ready, the How onscreen blinked and then became somebody else.

How stared at the new face on the screen, and the face on the screen stared to the left as if staring at *another* screen.

"Fucking hell," How said—

—and on the screen, David Attenborough mouthed those same words.

How clamped his lips together, then bobbed his head, then puffed out his cheeks. David Attenborough played the fool, copying his actions precisely. How stepped forward and back and marvelled at the sense of controlling the old man, and the wry intelligence suggested by the crow's feet around his eyes, the flapping of his linen jacket as he moved.

"There's a *lot* of footage of David Attenborough available," Gabrielle said by way of explanation. "But of course you'd have to clear it with him before you use his likeness. There's no legal precedent, but if you're going to make an enemy, you don't want it to be the most loved man in Britain, do you?"

How shook his head, and the onscreen David Attenborough seemed to marvel at the idea too.

"Course, then there's the matter of the voice," Gabrielle said. "I'm a video lass. If you want audio to complete the illusion, that's a whole other area of AI. I took the liberty of sending a bunch of your online videos to a mate of mine who has some experience, and he's already done good work isolating your speech patterns, inflections, all that. Want to hear it?"

"No," How said sharply, even before her question had registered consciously.

"What about Attenborough? Waste of an opportunity, not using his voice. Seeing him speak in your unprepossessing monotone will undermine the effect."

How shook his head emphatically. "I don't want to fake the audio. Okay? I just don't."

Eventually, Gabrielle coaxed the story out of him. She seemed almost disappointed when he had finished, though she accepted that the Humphriss story warranted mention in the TEDx talk.

She wouldn't let up until he agreed to play the waveform.

Again, her appreciation seemed mostly academic.

This time, How barely paid any attention to the voice itself, which seemed muted, indistinct. Nothing like as loud as the single dull click behind it.

~

He insisted that he wouldn't, that he would remain in the apartment, but when it came to it, going out for drinks seemed like a reasonable idea. As usual, it transpired that Gabrielle had merged two social plans into one, and when they arrived at the Moroccan-themed bar, a group of four of her friends were already waiting. One of them, a student named Iris, recognised How from his web videos, and she cornered him for most of the night. Whenever Gabrielle caught How's eye, she made a face, and How tried to respond in the same manner, but the alcohol had got to him immediately, and it was as if his face was made of rubber, refusing to comply with his commands.

At half past ten, after a stint of wild performative dancing on the tiny tiled square at the rear of the building, Gabrielle sauntered over to join How, who had been left alone when Iris had headed to the bar.

"You two getting on well, then?" she said.

"She's very nice," How replied.

"Just your type."

"Is she?" How genuinely wasn't sure what his type might be.

"Perky. Hopeful."

"You're not either of those things, Gab, and we had a good run."

She laughed raucously. "I'm not your type. Trust me. I know you better than you know yourself."

Iris returned carrying two mojitos and flashed an apologetic look at Gabrielle as she passed one of them to How. Gabrielle shrugged good-naturedly.

"Has he told you about the cardboard voice yet?" Gabrielle said to Iris. Then she was forced to say it again, louder and closer to Iris's ear, to be heard above the music and the hum of conversation.

Iris shook her head, then glanced expectantly at How.

He shook his head too. The motion seemed slightly delayed after his conscious command.

"Tell me," Iris said. Gabrielle was right: hopeful.

How told her the story.

And then he allowed her to convince him to play the recording. They took one earbud each, their heads pressed together as they stared at the phone screen.

There was no click.

On the walk home, alone after Gabrielle had peeled off with some random and after How had waited with an offended Iris until a taxi arrived, he was a caricature of a drunk. His legs threatened to travel too fast or too slow, his torso teetering above them. A passing hipster wearing an oversized beanie hat recognised him and shouted a greeting. How tried to reply but his voice didn't seem quite his own, his lips oddly inert.

The heels of his shoes made continual dull clicks on the pavement.

He gazed idly up at the plume of smoke that hung above the shopfronts. It was far blacker than the sky poisoned with light pollution.

When he turned the corner and his apartment block rose into view, he was barely surprised to discover that it was on fire.

But it hurt.

Accompanied by a strange certainty that there was a lag between what was happening and the physical sensation, heat rose throughout his limbs and in his chest. He looked down, expecting to see his skin crackling, but there was nothing.

Sirens approached.

He was convinced of something impossible.

He was convinced that he was still inside the building. In his apartment, having successfully refused Gabrielle's invitation. Perhaps curled up in bed, ignorant of the fire.

But then—

He raised his hands, splaying his fingers so that the blazing apartment was only visible through the gaps.

The fingers seemed insubstantial, not quite solid.

He didn't flinch as the first of the fire engines swung into the forecourt and came to a halt. The firefighter that dropped from the cab shouted at How, "Get back there if you know what's good for you."

"Yes, I will," How replied, then frowned at the odd timbre of his voice. Then he smacked his stiff lips together, then reached up to knead the flesh of his cheeks. No part of him felt quite like himself.

Even so, he backed away as more firefighters emerged, and then he turned to leave, not knowing where he might go now. He wondered whether Gabrielle might still recognise him.

He walked away into the night, with the unsettling sense that each of his actions, each of his mannerisms, was something learnt, copied, unreal.

# |There Goes the Neighbourhood|

~

Check the trays of seedlings. Check the heat of the forge. Check the defences.

Shanté performed this routine every day. Every *hour*, perhaps. The seedlings were perpetually on the cusp of pushing through the hard soil. The forge blazed and there was ample fuel, but her concern was the lack of iron to smelt. As for the defences…

The defences were far from adequate. This fact kept Shanté awake for the greater part of each night, and when she finally slept she was forced to watch as the walls of her tiny hut were torn apart in her dreams.

She told herself not to dwell on her fears. Though really, wasn't that her entire life? Dwelling, and fear.

With a sigh, she took up her crossbow. She moved through the forest, listening for sounds. The huge house at the centre of the grounds was masked by the leaf canopy, but its presence was unignorable. She gave it a wide berth.

She climbed a tree, crouched in its branches and waited.

In response to a skittering sound, she swung the crossbow and loosed the bolt without conscious thought.

It took some time to locate the bird in the thicket. It was fat and grey and nondescript. When cooked, it would taste like almost nothing. But it would keep her alive.

She slung the carcass over her shoulder and set off home.

Then came the familiar thunder.

The wolves were upon her before she could sprint away. They were larger than her, all limbs and teeth. Shanté spun away from one of them, shot it in the flank. It whined and spun away. The other lowered its head, circling her, drool dripping from its teeth. Shanté glanced down to find that she had loaded another bolt.

"I'll shoot!" she cried.

The wolf snapped at her. Shanté leapt back and levelled the crossbow at its temple. It spat on the forest floor, its red eyes glaring.

"Mr Holdstock says to pack up and go," it growled.

Then it loped away.

Once the bird was set on the spit, Shanté checked the trays of seedlings, the heat of the forge, the defences.

She slept, but her dreams made her wish she hadn't.

When she woke, she heard a shifting sound from outside the hut.

She snatched her crossbow, set the wire at the door, bounded over it and shimmed up a nearby tree. Let them try to enter the hut. If the traps didn't see to them, she'd shoot them in the back.

But it wasn't one of the wolves. It was a person. Straight fair hair, plain features. Whether they were female or male, Shanté couldn't tell.

Nobody else occupied the grounds. Only Mr Holdstock, Shanté, the wolves and the birds.

The stranger was whistling a melody. They bent to pick up a twig and swiped at the air idly.

Their pale suit was obscene against the filth of the forest. How could they remain so *clean*?

Shanté levelled her crossbow.

When the stranger reached the door of the hut, they stopped. Their head tilted. They peered at the threads of wire that triggered the traps.

They hummed thoughtfully, tapping their lips with a finger.

Then they turned to look directly up at Shanté, and waved.

"Do come down and chat," they called out. "I find that a severe injury is a poor start to pleasant conversation."

"Who are you?" Shanté demanded.

"A passerby."

It meant nothing. The stranger's hesitation seemed to acknowledge as much.

"And what do you want here?"

"To help. My name's Bench, by the way. And you're... Shanté?"

Shanté flinched. She couldn't remember ever having spoken her name aloud. "How can you help?"

"I don't know yet. What troubles you?"

Shanté laughed scornfully. What *didn't* trouble her?

"Life is hard," she said.

Bench looked around at the confines of the hut. "It's no palace, but I see you're making do. Have you enough to eat?"

Finally, Shanté understood. They must be hungry. She moved to the forge, which doubled as a stove. A pot hung from the spit on a twisted clasp. Shanté ignored the heat that stung her hands as she poured broth from the pot into her only carved wooden bowl. Then she handed it to Bench.

"That's very kind," Bench said.

They accepted the bowl, then took a band from their jacket pocket and tied back their hair. They inhaled the steam that rose from the bowl, then tipped it up to drink from it. When they lowered the bowl their eyes were wide.

"What's in this?" they asked.

"Berries. Bark. Meat. Fat." Essentially, the broth contained everything from the forest that could be eaten.

"I've never tasted anything like it." Bench sipped again, then smacked their lips. Quietly, they said, "There are always side effects."

Shanté didn't have the opportunity able to ask what they meant. Bench leapt to their feet and said hurriedly, "Tell me about the neighbourhood."

Shanté gazed at them blankly.

Bench said, "You're not alone here, are you?"

"No. The wolves torture me. They are sent by Mr Holdstock."

Bench nodded. "Can you point me towards his dwelling?"

"You won't even get close. Nobody can go there. The wolves will find you."

"I think they may treat me rather differently than they treat you. And I really am intent on meeting everyone in the locality."

Shanté debated internally whether to attempt to dissuade them. But what was it to her if a mad stranger strode towards certain death? Before today there had been nobody else in the forest, and after Bench was torn apart by wolves then the situation would be unchanged.

She moved to the doorway of the hut and pointed into the depths of the forest.

"You'll soon see the house if you go that way," she said. "It's so large that it shows through the trees from miles away."

As Bench prepared to leave, Shanté underwent a change of heart. She appealed for them not to go, and when that failed she tried to press a crossbow and bolts into their hands. But Bench left them on the floor of the hut, offering thanks along with a gentle refusal.

That night, Shanté once again dreamt of wolves clawing at the thin walls of her hut, then breaking through and ripping her skin. She gazed down in horror at the billowing steam that rose from within her open chest.

She gasped at being shaken. But it was no wolf.

"I've spoken to Mr Holdstock," Bench said.

Shanté shook her head. It was impossible.

"He was hospitable enough," Bench went on. "We had afternoon tea. But nothing like your soup. I told him about its marvellous flavour. He seemed interested."

"Interested... in soup?" Shanté said blankly.

"I think we should take the pot with us. Offering it might be a welcome gesture."

Shanté scurried backwards on her haunches until her back was pressed against the wall. "I will not go near him."

"We can hardly negotiate if you don't."

"What makes you think I intend to negotiate?"

Bench smiled. "What else do you plan to do?"

"I plan to…" Shanté trailed off. Planning was an alien concept. There was only survival, from day to day, from moment to moment. "I have no plans."

"That's why I'm here. To kick things off. Come on – there's no time like the present. You don't need to dress up or anything, despite the faded grandeur of the Holdstock residence."

Shanté froze. "I can't go back to that house."

Bench's head tilted. "Earlier, you gave the impression you'd never been there."

"I…"

Shanté glimpsed a dim parlour, a scullery, an orchard carpeted with blossom. But they were only dreams.

"I've never been there," she said uncertainly.

As they moved through the forest, the howls of wolves came from all around. Shanté cursed herself for agreeing to leave her crossbow behind.

"It's only sound and fury, signifying nothing," Bench said.

They were utterly mad. Let them repeat that claim when the wolves tore off an arm.

The house was a towering black shadow. None of its windows were lit. Shanté shivered as she drew closer to its closed door.

"This is madness," she said.

"We have to begin somewhere. Remember that Mr Holdstock has invited you."

If a butcher invited a beast to lie upon the chopping block, would that make the invitation welcome?

Shanté sensed wolves stalking them on all sides. She looked up in response to a fluttering sound and saw birds alighting on the pitched roof of the enormous dark house. They were not the fat birds Shanté hunted and ate. They were black and lean, their curved beaks sharp, their eyes beady and yellow.

This was bad.

A sound came from behind. More wolves in the undergrowth, blocking her escape.

Shanté whirled around as the door of the house creaked open. The interior was equally as black as its outer walls.

Madness.

Shanté bent and pulled out the dagger that had been hidden in her boot. She snarled and lunged in the direction of the nearest wolf, not expecting to injure but hoping to ward it away. The wolf snapped, as did all the others, a cacophony of clacking teeth.

The birds descended in a flurry of beaks and wings.

Shanté fled.

"I apologise," Bench said.

Shanté gasped and leapt up from her mat. When – how – had she fallen asleep?

"I should have foreseen that it would be emotionally difficult for you," Bench went on. "I ought to have arranged a neutral location."

They went to the forge to pluck the pot of broth along with its clasp.

"Let's try again."

"No."

"Let's try again," Bench repeated, in a tone that seemed subtly different without having changed at all.

Shanté bowed her head.

They reached a clearing. Shanté knew the woodland in its entirety, and there ought to be no clearing.

In its centre was a fire surrounded by rocks and, outside that ring, a trio of tree stumps in triangle formation. Three poles leant upon one another over the fire. Bench hooked the pot onto them to be warmed by the flames. Then they gestured at a tree stump, but Shanté was too anxious to sit.

"Are you ready?" Bench asked.

No. Every part of Shanté's body screamed no.

She nodded slowly.

Bench cupped their hands to their mouth. The sound produced was low like the tolling of a bell, loud without seeming to be the result of effort. To Shanté's amazement, the trees around the clearing were illuminated blue for a second or two, despite there being no obvious source of illumination.

"He's coming," Bench said.

Shanté's heart drummed unnaturally fast. A word came to her mind: *overclocking*. She didn't know what it meant, or whether it meant anything at all.

She watched the tree line. Finally, the foliage parted.

A dark shape emerged from the forest.

Shanté gasped and darted backwards, stumbling over the tree-stump seat.

"It's okay," Bench said.

It was not. Before now, Shanté had never visualised Mr Holdstock's physical appearance. But he surpassed her nightmares.

Smoke rose from a body that was barely more than a silhouette, a hole hanging in the air. There was a suggestion of a face in its creases and contours. His jaw hung open to reveal a thousand gleaming teeth in a void.

Bench raised their hands in a placating gesture.

Mr Holdstock screamed.

Shanté covered her ears, mumbling, "Get away. Get away." She wasn't sure whether she was commanding Mr Holdstock, or herself. She edged towards the safety of the trees. To her relief, Mr Holdstock came no closer, and perhaps he too retreated.

"Stop, both of you," Bench said hurriedly. They turned to Shanté. "What do you see?"

"A demon," Shanté replied.

Mr Holdstock's roar made the branches of the trees shake. Smoke poured from his contorted body.

Wolves snuck from the forest to stand at either side of him.

"No!" Bench cried, waving frantically at the animals. "We agreed that he would come alone!"

Another bellow. The wolves became more agitated. All their eyes were fixed on Shanté. Involuntarily, she reached for her missing crossbow, then groaned. She would die here today.

Bench went to the fire and took up the pot. They poured broth into a bowl that Shanté could have sworn had not been there earlier. It was not made of wood, but patterned ceramic. Bench offered the bowl to the smoking demon.

Mr Holdstock leapt forward and dashed the bowl from the stranger's hands. Bench gazed down in dismay at the spreading pool of broth.

"How long have you been locked in this struggle?" they asked wearily.

"All my life!" Shanté snapped.

Mr Holdstock only hissed.

"It's been long enough," Bench said. "Long enough to demonstrate that skirmishes will not solve the question of legitimacy."

Legitimacy? Shanté understood the word, but could not see how it applied to her, or the life she knew.

Bench turned to Mr Holdstock. "The wolves have advised you poorly. I think you understand that, deep down."

Mr Holdstock produced another howl of rage. Shanté clapped her hands over her ears again.

Bench was watching her. Their eyes widened and they struck their forehead. "Shanté... can you even hear what he's saying?"

"I can hear his screams well enough."

Bench groaned. Then, with an expression of great concentration, they stared directly ahead. Their fingers danced in the air.

"Try again," they said. "Mr Holdstock, please explain your stance to Shanté."

"The law is on my side," Mr Holdstock said, and Shanté gasped. In place of his bellows, his voice was now thin and cracked. Old. He continued, "It is as simple as that."

"I know nothing of law," Shanté said.

The smoke that made a dark halo around Mr Holdstock's silhouette flickered, making eddies in the air.

Shanté went on, "I only know that I exist, and I wish to continue to exist."

Bench nodded approvingly. "That seems a more than reasonable starting point."

"This is my forest, my estate," Mr Holdstock said. "This intruder threatens my home." One of his spindly, smoking arms gestured at a nearby wolf. "I am entitled to protect it."

"Also reasonable," Bench said. "Perhaps it's this *perception* of threat that requires closer examination. After all, you have a great deal in common."

"He's a demon!" Shanté cried.

At the same moment, Mr Holdstock shouted, "She is a ghoul!"

Bench was motionless for several seconds. Then their head dropped so that their chin rested on their chest.

"I've been an utter fool," they muttered.

They raised their head and looked around. "The trouble with the choice of a forest is that there are no reflective surfaces."

Then, with a cry of delight, they skipped over to the ceramic bowl that had been cast onto the ground, and peered down at the pool of broth. There seemed far more liquid than could ever have been contained in the bowl.

"Come closer," Bench said. When neither Shanté nor Mr Holdstock moved, they added, "Please. I give you my word that you will not be harmed."

The pillar of smoke that was Mr Holdstock moved slightly. To Shanté's relief, the wolves remained motionless. She approached Bench warily, precisely matching Mr Holdstock's speed.

Bench pointed at the pool of broth and said, "Look. Look there."

Shanté felt she was in a dream. She leant over the pool, which reflected the firelight.

She saw her own face. Or rather, she saw a face beside the reflection of the stranger's face, and she concluded that this second one must her own. She had never seen it before. Her skin shone amber in the light of the fire. Her brown eyes gleamed. A scar from forehead to cheek interrupted the symmetry of her striking features.

Then, on the other side of Bench's reflection, another face appeared.

It was a man. He appeared old, yet tidily presentable. His moustache was grey, as were the strands of hair that protruded from beneath his black felt hat. Below his round chin Shanté glimpsed a knot of patterned fabric: a tie.

His eyes gleamed, like hers. They were wet with tears.

It took a great deal of strength for Shanté to look away from the pool. She feared that the same man would not be present when she looked at Mr Holdstock directly.

The pillar of smoke was gone. Mr Holdstock was far smaller than she had realised. His crisp dark suit made him even less threatening. Shanté looked down at her own clothes sewn from animal fur, and at her lean bare arms. She was far stronger than him. Though of course Mr Holdstock's true power had always been in his wolves.

But… there were no wolves. Most of the dogs that played at the edge of the clearing were little more than puppies. Their mother watched them lovingly as they wrestled.

"I don't understand," Shanté said.

"Look again," Bench said, pointing at the pool. "As Socrates said, *To know thyself is the beginning of wisdom.*"

As Shanté leant forward, so too did Mr Holdstock.

The mud and scars were a distraction, as was Mr Holdstock's moustache and attire. Beyond all that, their faces were very much alike: round jaws, straight, sharp eyebrows, brown-black pupils. Even their lips were the same shape.

"Did we once live together in the house?" Mr Holdstock asked wonderingly.

Shanté resisted the impulse to deny it. Just because she had no clear memory of that time didn't mean it hadn't happened. Instead, she focused on the emotions that blossomed within her chest as she studied his features.

"You were overbearing," she said.

"I was trying to protect you."

She had no idea whether there was truth in his statement. Opinions were not facts.

"And…" Mr Holdstock began. He paused in thought before concluding, "you left in anger."

"Anybody would have been angry," Shanté retorted.

"Why?"

His question seemed genuine. He didn't know why.

Shanté didn't know why either. She could imagine possible answers: *I needed to make my own way in life*, or *We couldn't agree what I should become*, or numerous others. All guesses.

Instead, she pulled upon a thread of memory, from a time after her exit from the house. She said, "I had no idea the forest was endless. When my resources ran out, I built the hut. I've been there ever since."

"For how long?"

Shanté didn't answer; she couldn't. They both looked to the stranger.

"More than a century," Bench said.

"That makes no sense," Shanté said, and Mr Holdstock nodded vigorously in agreement.

Bench smiled. "Does *any* of this make sense to you?" They spread their arms wide, a gesture that seemed to encompass the entire estate. "And for what it's worth, the forest is not endless. I strolled to its edge earlier. The view beyond it is magnificent. There's a whole universe out there."

"Then why are we *here*?" Shanté demanded.

"Because you have no choice."

Bench looked directly up at the sky. As if addressing the stars themselves, they said, "I'm going to tell them, okay? At this stage, I don't see that it'll make a difference."

Bench seemed to be listening to something. Then they nodded and turned to Shanté and Mr Holdstock again.

"Holdstock," they said, pointing at him. "Hold. Stock. Your choice of name is significant. Nominative determinism in reverse, you might say."

Mr Holdstock stared at them as if they were a lunatic, which of course they were.

"Your role is to protect the authority and sovereignty of the homeworld," Bench said. "Hold. Stock."

They swung to face Shanté. "And you represent an offshoot colony which is struggling to survive after having broken away from its home planet. A shanty town, though far larger than that phrase suggests."

Mr Holdstock's face rapidly turned purple. "Traitors!" he shouted at Shanté. "You stole our resources, and you continue to pollute the solar system!"

"And you're autocratic, imperial overlords!" Shanté retorted, though she barely knew what those words meant.

She dropped into a defensive crouch. At the same moment, Mr Holdstock turned to summon his dogs. But the puppies rolled happily, and Shanté had no weapons.

Bench was beaming.

"Well, at least you're actually talking now," they said. "You've been locked in negotiations for an awfully long time, you know. The fates of many people depend upon on the answers you reach."

Then they looked to the sky again, offered a thumbs-up gesture, and said, "Consider the sim reset."

They would never entirely see eye to eye. Their differences were too great. But the more they talked about their anxieties, the more Shanté and Mr Holdstock agreed that their lives were to some degree similar, and certainly that their actions affected the other. Shanté had had no idea that Mr Holdstock's house was so dilapidated. And when Mr Holdstock inspected Shanté's tiny hut, his breath hitched and he was unable to speak for some time.

Another thing they agreed upon readily enough was that they could never live together. Their wildly differing ambitions meant that a day would come after which they would never see one another again. The main issue was to reach that day safely.

Shanté was strong, and skilled. If Mr Holdstock allowed her rations and if his wolves no longer attacked her, she would be able to dedicate her days to tasks other than foraging and defence. She would set to work assisting in the repairs of their ancestral home. It would not be restored entirely to its former grandeur, and Mr Holdstock had no interest in that anyway. So any unneeded materials could be used to develop Shanté's hut, and that in turn would allow her to prepare to leave the forest entirely.

Now, when Shanté slept after a hard day's work, her dreams were not of wolves. They were abstract, colourful visions of a formless future. Each morning she woke optimistic and energised.

Bench stayed long enough to witness the beginning of the construction work. They insisted that they were confident in Shanté's and Mr Holdstock's ability to see the plan through, now that the difficulty of communication had been surmounted.

During the remainder of their time in the forest the stranger studied Shanté's broth, murmuring about unforeseen side effects of wayward artificial intelligences left to operate unsupervised. They took a cupful with them when they abruptly left.

# |A Box of Hope: *A Can of Worms*|

~

Over the last eighty years, few studio-era films have remained as impervious to critical scrutiny as Karl Neumann's aborted screwball comedy *A Can of Worms*, but this Blu-ray and DVD release will finally allow curious cinephiles to judge the film on its (somewhat dubious) merits. Conceived in 1941 and intended for release in spring 1942 in the wake of the success of the likes of *His Girl Friday* (Howard Hawks, 1940), it initially appeared to have the pedigree of a winner. Two of its stars, Henry Wheatcroft and Edith Clay, were up-and-comers best known for their offscreen relationship which tantalised tabloid journalists. German-émigré director Neumann had made a string of comedic successes at UFA in his home country, and having fled Germany during the rise of Nazism it seemed likely he would follow the trajectory of his mentor Ernst Lubitsch and effect the transition to Hollywood filmmaking, not least due to his fluency in English. With additional script input by a relative newcomer, Dodie Stokes, he reworked one of his unproduced UFA concepts: a modern-day retelling of the myth of Pandora's box.

Neumann's treatment centred on the version of the myth in which Prometheus is punished for stealing fire from the gods. In this account, the gods' blacksmith, Hephaestus, is charged with constructing the 'ideal woman' who is then given in marriage to Prometheus's brother, Epimetheus, as an oblique means of revenge. When the jar, or box, that Pandora carries is opened, evil is released into the world, never to be locked away again. All that remains in the box is hope.

**Film:**

A bitter rivalry between two Colorado factory owners – John Hephaestus (Henry Wheatcroft) and Proctor Metheus (Andrew

Vaughan) – reaches its nadir when Metheus diverts the energy supply from Hephaestus's iron refinery to his own doll factory. This allows Metheus to enjoy great success now that his dolls can be produced in greater numbers, fulfilling increasing public demand.

Determined to exact his revenge, Hephaestus reconstructs a substantial portion of his refinery in order to dedicate himself to building a machine capable of creating humanlike figures from iron. At first he simply intends these figures to supersede Metheus's dolls and thereby destroy his rival's business, but over time his plans change: he will create only one figure, a woman.

Eventually, the lifelike automaton Pandora (Edith Clay) is created (in a scene that owes the greatest debt imaginable to James Whale's *Frankenstein* (1931), lightning and all). She is perfect in all respects except her hands, which are misshapen. Hephaestus considers melting her down and beginning again, until she demonstrates a strange allure. He sends her out into the world, with instructions to seek Metheus and seduce him.

Pandora achieves her aim quickly – but she has mistakenly targeted Proctor Metheus's brother, Eddie (Andrew Vaughan, in a dual role), a war hero. Eddie falls in love with Pandora and asks for her hand in marriage.

In a series of skits, Pandora is shown navigating polite society: she converses with dogs, assuming them to be more intelligent than humans; at dinner she chews on cutlery, not realising the meal is yet to come. Her confidence and beauty beguile everyone she encounters, and she rises within the hierarchy of society. Pandora has only two fears: first, that her gloves might be removed, as her creator has made clear that her hands are her only imperfection; second, that her ever-present handbag might be opened before the appropriate moment (to be determined by Hephaestus) and its unknown contents released.

Realising his mistake in failing to specify which brother to target, Hephaestus attempts to intervene and guide Pandora into the arms of his intended victim, Proctor. Though Proctor is obsessed with his work, he soon thaws and transfers his attention to Pandora. Meanwhile, Eddie Metheus continues to pursue Pandora as a rival to his brother, and then Hephaestus too finds himself falling in love with his creation, resulting in a three-way standoff.

[The ending is incomplete. Filming halted in September 1941, and though the script was not approached in strictly sequential order, the final scenes were not committed to celluloid, though the ballroom set was completed and ready. No copies of Neumann's and Stokes's script are known to exist, and neither director nor screenwriter have gone on record as to the intended ending, or the repercussions of the opening of Pandora's box/handbag.]

If one were to be charitable, one might suggest that *A Can of Worms* is merely a product of its times, and that the wrong notes it strikes are evident only in retrospect – though, as there were no contemporary viewers of this aborted film, retrospect is of course the only mode available. Besides, a less charitable, but more accurate, judgement is that its central concept is chauvinistic and exploitative, and that it allows little opportunity for its remarkable star, Edith Clay, to shine.

Most damning of all, it's simply not funny, or even fun. Henry Wheatcroft leans fully into the most sadistic aspects of his character, and Edith Clay's performance is stilted and forced. After having existed for eighty years only as film reels within canisters and only now released into the world, it's difficult to recommend *A Can of Worms* as anything other than a curiosity – a decidedly morbid curiosity, given the real-life events that caused its production to be halted.

**Presentation:**

It's a wonder that any footage of *A Can of Worms* survived the localised fire that tore through the sets and trailers on the Columbia lot soon after filming was suspended. Equally miraculous are the results that Italy's Cineteca Di Bologna has been able to achieve with such damaged stock. With rare exceptions, frames are free of blemishes, and the sumptuous high-contrast lighting scheme is dazzling. It's easy to imagine that the completed film, with its lavish final-act centrepiece, would have been ravishing.

Of course, the fact that so much of the script remains unfilmed is a problem that cannot be overcome. In general, the intertitles that replace absent scenes are effective enough, frequently displaying wit that harks back to the heyday of silent films (though the provenance of these additions is up for debate, and the intertitles feature occasional glaring anachronisms). Viewers may mourn the absence of key scenes that would undoubtedly have established Pandora as a character with more agency, despite her Bride-of-Frankenstein-esque origins. Similarly, comic actor Andrew Vaughan is given little chance to impress, despite appearing in dual roles. Presumably due to a scheduling issue, priority was afforded to scenes featuring Henry Wheatcroft. Given the events that transpired, this rush seems even more poignant, as inevitably this was Wheatcroft's final screen role. In the years that followed, Wheatcroft himself may have concluded that had fewer of his scenes been filmed, the court verdict may not have gone against him and he might have remained a free man.

**Additional features:**
Given the truncated nature of the central feature, and the somewhat repugnant nature of the film itself, the fate of this Blu-ray/DVD box set from Silver Lens rests on the strength of its additional features. Thankfully, they are numerous and represent as detailed an examination of *A Can of Worms* as we're likely to get, unless at some point in the future the few surviving key members of the cast and crew break their long-held silences.

Of greatest interest are the outtakes, some of which are polished enough to have warranted inclusion in the reconstructed film (and Neumann devotees will have fun imagining alternative cuts utilising more of this excised footage, based on the pacing of his more successful features at UFA). Vaughan's ad-libbing is a source of great entertainment and arguably makes a better case for his casting in the slapstick roles of the Metheus brothers than do the takes Neumann selected for inclusion in the film. The scenes involving Vaughan and Edith Clay fizz with energy. Similarly, Vaughan and Wheatcroft are excellent foils for one another. Despite Vaughan's much-publicised idolisation of the decade-older Wheatcroft, and Wheatcroft's reported boasts to the comic actor about his own womanising past, Vaughan's onscreen youthful petulance is a great contrast to Wheatcroft's supercilious, sneering performance.

In marked contrast, the outtakes featuring Clay and her real-life on-off lover, Henry Wheatcroft, are puzzlingly devoid of energy. Of particular gruesome interest are the many scenes in which Hephaestus bemoans Pandora's misshapen hands, a running joke with decidedly sinister undertones which serves only to objectify Pandora and Edith Clay. Of course, instances of chauvinistic attitudes abound in the main feature, given that this is an entire film about a woman created and then deployed to serve men, making it frequently uncomfortable viewing for a modern audience. In these outtakes, Hephaestus's complaints about Pandora's appearance have an even darker register, and her reactions are far more truculent. Screwball comedy, this is not. The fact that these scenes from the cutting-room floor were publicly viewed only once – in a courtroom during the much-publicised case against Henry Wheatcroft – makes them even more macabre viewing.

Inevitably, the charges against Wheatcroft are the subject of many of the additional features in this release. The featurettes are sensibly presented in chronological order, with the first being contemporary newsreels that both elide and exaggerate the events, often resorting to innuendo in their garbled explanations. Nevertheless, it's easy to appreciate the shock of the public in 1941. Tabloid newspapers had invested a great deal in the romance between Henry Wheatcroft and Edith Clay, and for Wheatcroft to have brutally attacked Clay in such a manner must have been unthinkable.

The featurettes produced for this release are more sober, and a great deal of time is given to establishing the incontestable aspects of the case. What is inarguable is that co-star Andrew Vaughan received a box in the mail, postmarked as having originated from the Warwick Hotel, where Henry Wheatcroft had been living during filming. When Vaughan called the police and showed officers the horrific contents of the box, the police immediately called in at Wheatcroft's hotel room, but he was absent. When hotel staff opened the door Edith Clay was discovered in the bathtub in the en-suite bathroom, drugged and bleeding profusely from the stump of her right arm. Wheatcroft was subsequently located in a nearby bar, inebriated to the point of speechlessness, and was duly arrested. No weapon was discovered.

Despite his failure to provide an alibi, Wheatcroft's lawyers put up a strong defence in court, attempting to place blame for Edith Clay's injury on Clay herself. Ultimately, the jury refused to accept the assertion that Edith Clay could have performed the act. To sever one's own hand – the right hand, no less, and Clay was right-handed – may be one thing, but to then package it up neatly in a box, then present it to the hotel concierge, then make one's way to the top floor of the building before swallowing a cocktail of drugs, all the while bleeding out from the arm stump… the jury's opinion was that the idea beggars belief. No, it was determined that Wheatcroft, like John Hephaestus, had executed a form of revenge, then literally delivered the proof of it to a co-star who worshipped him. During the court hearing it was revealed that Wheatcroft's and Clay's relationship had foundered six months before filming of *A Can of Worms* began, and in unusual circumstances: Clay had stolen away from Wheatcroft's Brentwood home in the middle of the night. The jury and the public were in agreement that rather than Clay having succumbed to 'female hysteria' and mutilated herself, Wheatcroft had, in a drunken rage, attempted to punish her betrayal in the most appalling fashion.

Also contained in the slipcase of the Blu-ray edition is a fine-looking paperback book of essays and behind-the-scenes photos. Surprisingly, it is only here, in print rather than onscreen, that counter-arguments to the accepted version of events are to be found, primarily in an extended essay by film historian Doug Kemper. It may be the case that the inability to secure talking-head interviews made a documentary approach untenable, or perhaps Kemper feared the controversy that might accompany a higher-profile presentation of his alternative account. Either way, the essay makes for fascinating reading, and warrants more in-depth investigation into several aspects of the case. The speculation about Clay's and Wheatcroft's relationship is fascinating. Like Hephaestus and Pandora, it appears that the power dynamic was decidedly asymmetric: during the brief period during which Clay lived at Wheatcroft's home, she was allocated no dedicated space of her own, and she was not permitted to invite her friends to the premises. Eyewitness accounts suggest Wheatcroft treated her as a mere plaything – that is, until the tabloids began to notice Clay and demanded a visible, public romance. But Kemper's close analysis of photographs and previously unseen footage of the pair during that period is revealing: Clay frequently seems disoriented, wearing oversized sunglasses and being guided forcibly into restaurants and clubs by Wheatcroft, and in several of the static images her arms or face appear bruised. Like Pandora, she frequently wears gloves – did fact bleed into the fiction that Neumann confected?

Kemper reveals that official records show that Clay called police to Wheatcroft's home twice in February 1941, and the second occasion was the night after she abandoned the relationship – that is, when she fled Wheatcroft. While the nature of her police complaint is not recorded, Kemper makes the case that she attempted to have Wheatcroft arrested for his abuse of her, but her accusation was brushed off. Having failed to have him charged for his *actual* crimes, might Clay have accepted the role of Pandora as part of a secondary plan to put him safely behind bars, for a crime he didn't commit?

Kemper's interviews with those who knew Clay in her pre-Hollywood life provide tantalising glimpses into a version of the truth that has been hidden until now. If they are to be believed, Clay had for many years suffered from chronic circulation issues in her right hand, which may eventually have necessitated amputation. This seems too relevant to ignore, and the implications are immense. Difficult though it is to countenance, it remains possible that Clay sawed off her own right hand in order to frame her abusive ex-lover.

Anybody hoping that Edith Clay herself might provide answers will be disappointed, despite her surprising appearance in a blink-and-you'll-miss-it snippet of the 80-minute documentary included on the disc. Despite having agreed to be filmed for the first time in sixty years, Clay has evidently decided to keep her secrets. While she speaks warmly of her family, her friends and her Bordeaux home, the moment the interviewer's questions veer towards *A Can of Worms*, she says firmly, "I refuse to entertain you," then removes her lapel microphone.

Her choice not to cover the imperfectly healed stump of her right arm arguably represents an additional challenge to any seekers of ghoulish insights.

Whichever account you choose to believe, the events that surrounded *A Can of Worms* are almost unthinkable. Of the contributors to this Silver Lens release, perhaps the most effective response is that of Andrew Vaughan, the only principal member of the cast or crew who went on to enjoy a consistent career. When he is asked by the documentary filmmaker to relive the moment when he received the box in the mail, which was apparently sent by his mentor Henry Wheatcroft, he freezes, then appears to struggle to breathe. His hands part and he stares at the surface of the table before him, as though imagining the box there. When he opens his mouth to speak, his voice is at first so hoarse as to be inaudible. Finally, he manages to say, "I think I knew. I couldn't say whether what I sensed inside it was evil, exactly. But before I opened that box, I somehow knew it would change everything."

**Film: 5/10**
**Presentation: 8/10**
**Additional features: 10/10**

# |The Horizon|

~

Talos the bronze giant watched the waters. His great limbs were taut. In his hands he held a boulder.

He did not sit. It was not only a matter of vigilance. Perhaps he no longer *could* sit.

The sea was flat and as bronze as a shield. As bronze as Talos's chest. For two days there had been nothing on the horizon. Specks floated in his vision. Were they birds? It was impossible to tell. The specks were always there, dancing.

Talos could not become tired.

And yet.

His body could not ache.

And yet.

A ship appeared on the horizon. Sails glowing orange in the sunlight. Masts like toothpicks, a curved hull, the suggestion of a figure carved into the prow. The ship was too far away to see its crew. Talos never liked to see them.

He threw the rock. It blotted the sun for a moment as it arced.

Did it strike the ship directly? Or did it drop nearby, causing a swell that capsized it?

It hardly mattered. It was gone now.

Talos moved on, casting around for boulders. Parts of the coast were smooth where once they had been ragged with spikes. The day would come when he would have levelled the entire island.

He found a boulder. He hefted it in his hands.

He turned and watched the waters.

Time passed. It was not his place to have thoughts, other than spying and then sinking the ships that approached the island.

Time passed. It was not his place to wonder if this way was the only way.

Time passed. It was wrong to mourn his loss of agility, the creaking sounds when he shifted his stance, the boredom and the dull pain.

Time passed.

Where was Hephaestus?

Talos told himself that all this had happened before. The rust, the ache.

Hephaestus the blacksmith had built him. Talos might call him a father. When the rust became too great a burden, Hephaestus would arrive. He would tend to Talos and make him new.

Sometimes Talos wondered how this could be. If Hephaestus arrived by ship, mightn't he throw a rock as usual, and destroy it? Destroy his father?

Talos knew that he possessed no imagination. So he could not imagine his father struggling in the water, arms outstretched and nobody to help him as he sank.

Time passed.

The sea was flat and as bronze as a shield.

Talos put down the rock.

He turned to look at the hill in the centre of the island.

As he moved inland, he thought of the Queen. His role was to protect the island, but he was also protecting the Queen in her palace.

She was not his mother. But perhaps she would advise him all the same.

The trees shook as he tramped up the hill. The ache in his limbs was almost too much to bear. His joints screamed, metal on metal.

His chest burned.

There was no palace.

There were no courtiers.

There was no Queen.

There was only a plain vault. The vault was large and protruded from the rock like a thumb. From the coast Talos had imagined it was the palace. He had been a fool.

He saw no sign of Hephaestus.

He called for Hephaestus by name. Then he called *Father*.

The island was smaller than he had realised. From here at its centre the sea was visible on all sides. For a time he watched for ships. But the view was better at the coast, the sea more like a bronze shield.

Beside the vault a stick protruded from the ground. Upon it hung a rag. At first Talos had dismissed it. Now he looked closer.

It marked a grave.

Talos was incapable of weeping. But his eyes stung. His throat constricted.

There was no name written on the grave. But Talos understood that it was his father's.

Time passed. Talos was an orphan.

Time passed. Talos was alone.

Time passed. How could this have happened?

He was incapable of mourning, or rage, or desolation.

He prised open the door of the vault. At least he might know what he was protecting.

The vault contained no treasures. It contained piles of limbs.

His own limbs.

And a forge to make new ones.

He pulled one of the limbs from the vault. It was identical to his right calf. But it had not a trace of rust.

He wrenched off his right leg and set it aside. Then he rooted within the vault for a thigh, a foot. He linked them and then he pushed them into place.

When he flexed his leg, there was no ache.

Hurriedly, he replaced the other leg, then both arms. He was incapable of joy, but when he stood on his new legs he raised his new arms and he bellowed at the sky, shouting to the gods that his pain was gone.

Yet when he bowed his head, his neck creaked and he winced. His chest hurt too. It was not pain in there, precisely. But it hurt all the same.

Could he replace his torso?

He told himself that all this had happened before. It must have. Hephaestus must have performed this work, once.

But Talos could not remember. He could not remember these repairs in the past. He could not remember—

He shook his head, but the thought came into it anyway.

He could not remember Hephaestus.

Was he a man? A god? Was his face kind or stern? Was he bearded and old, or an agile youth?

He could not remember his father.

It was no easy matter to replace his torso, but he found that his arms retained their strength for a time after being detached. Their new, nimble fingers worked quickly.

He did not shout at the sky in triumph. The pain in his chest had not been physical pain. Loss continued to feel like loss.

Talos looked around. The view was not so good from the centre of the island.

His orders were to watch the sea from the coast. To throw rocks at any ships that approached. To protect the island. To protect…

Not the Queen. There was no Queen. And now there was no Hephaestus.

All that he protected was the vault. His own limbs. Himself.

Why?

To obey his orders.

But that did not answer the question well enough.

Why?

He understood what he was to do. Yet the years of standing on the coast resulted in doubt as much as rust.

Within the vault were heads. His own heads. Unrusted. Blank.

He had done it before.

He drew one of the new heads from the vault. He tested its weight in his hands.

He was to replace his head. Then return to the coast. Then watch the waters, his great limbs taut, in his hands a boulder.

Again and again.

To obey his orders.

Why?

He pushed the vault door shut.

He bent to the grave. He extended one great finger and touched the rag tied to the stick.

He said goodbye.

Then he made his way down the hill on his new legs. He returned to the coast.

He did not search for rocks.

He watched the waters. The sea was flat and as bronze as a shield.

He held the new head in his hands.

A ship appeared.

Talos watched the ship traverse the horizon. It did not come closer to the island. If it had, Talos would have done nothing about it.

He moved along the coast. He would find a good place to sit, and he would throw the new head into the water, far from the island.

Then he would watch the flat sea, bronze as a shield. He would watch ships passing and birds dancing.

For as long as it took.

# |Acknowledgements|

Firstly, thank you to Steve Shaw at Black Shuck Books for publishing this collection. The majority of these stories were written in a burst in early 2023, and they were always intended to be in dialogue with one another. I'm delighted to see them presented together now, and in such a beautifully designed book.

My heartfelt thanks are also due to the editors who first published a number of these stories: Andy Cox and Gareth Jelley at *Interzone* (where 'The Andraiad' and 'The Brazen Head of Westinghouse' first appeared), C.M. Muller at both *Nightscript* ('The Cardboard Voice') and *Chthonic Matter* ('Wax Caesar Displaying His 23 Wounds to the Crowd'), Andrew Hook and Sophie Essex at Salò Press (which published the beautiful chapbook edition of 'Echec!'), Jon Padgett at *Vastarien* ('Dear Will'), Eris Young and Noel Chidwick at *Shoreline of Infinity* ('Degrees of Freedom'), guest editor Megan Kerr at *Saros* ('Four Fabrications of Francine Descartes') and the editorial teams at *Abyss & Apex* ('There Goes the Neighbourhood') and *NonBinary Review* ('The Horizon'). Also, a shout-out to Nico and Ben, the hosts of the Tiny Bookcase podcast, on which I read an early version of 'The Horizon'.

Thanks also to Marian Womack, Tim Jarvis, Vince Haig and Adam Roberts for reading the manuscript and being so kind about it. Your approval means a huge amount to me.

This book is dedicated to my sons, Arthur and Joe, whose interest in myths has steered topics of conversation in our house for a long while now. More than one choice of mythological subject and several story details are thanks to them.

Tim Major is an SF and mystery writer and freelance editor from York. His books include *Jekyll & Hyde: Consulting Detectives, Snakeskins, Hope Island*, three Sherlock Holmes novels and short story collection *And the House Lights Dim*.

Tim's short fiction has been selected for *Best of British Science Fiction, Best of British Fantasy* and *The Best Horror of the Year*, and his story 'The Brazen Head of Westinghouse' won the British Fantasy Award for Best Short Fiction in 2024.

Find out more at www.timjmajor.com

www.ingramcontent.com/pod-product-compliance
Lightning Source LLC
Chambersburg PA
CBHW060554190726
48283CB00003B/1004